W0043147

PENGUIN BOOKS
STORYWALLAH

Neelesh Misra is a lyricist, radio storyteller, journalist and writer. He is the founder and editor of *Gaon Connection*, India's biggest rural media platform, and the founder of Content Project, home to some of India's best emerging writers, collectively called the Mandali.

His exceptionally popular shows on radio and digital platforms include *Yaadon ka Idiot Box* (Big FM), *The Neelesh Misra Show* (Red FM), *Qisson ka Kona*, *Time Machine* and *Kahaani Express* (Saavn App). Neelesh is also one of Bollywood's prominent lyricists, the author of five books and two-time winner of the Ramnath Goenka Award for Excellence in Journalism.

If you wish to join Neelesh Misra's Mandali, send an original story in any Indian language to mandli@contentproject.in.

To connect directly with Neelesh, download his spoken and video content app 'Mic' or follow these verified pages and handles:
Facebook: @TheNeeleshMisraPage
Twitter and Instagram: @neeleshmisra
YouTube: Neelesh Misra

Storywallah

Neelesh Misra's Mandali

Translated from the Hindi by Khila Bisht

PENGUIN BOOKS

An imprint of Penguin Random House

PENGUIN BOOKS

USA | Canada | UK | Ireland | Australia
New Zealand | India | South Africa | China | Singapore

Penguin Books is part of the Penguin Random House group of companies
whose addresses can be found at global.penguinrandomhouse.com

Published by Penguin Random House India Pvt. Ltd
4th Floor, Capital Tower 1, MG Road,
Gurugram 122 002, Haryana, India

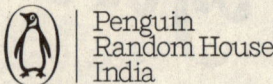

First published in Penguin Books by Penguin Random House India 2018

Copyright © Content Project Pvt. Ltd. for Neelesh Misra 2018
English translation copyright © Khila Bisht 2018

ISBN 9780143445777

Typeset in Bembo Std by Manipal Digital Systems, Manipal

Printed at Repro India Limited

CONTENTS

WILDFLOWER

Kanchan Pant

Nemat's breath quickened as the taxi snaked up the narrow hill road. There was no dip in the air's oxygen level, but she was finding it hard to breathe. Neither the cool wind coming in through the window nor the sweet Kumaoni music that filled the taxi like the sound of a mountain waterfall could allay her restlessness. She had been so small when Ma had taken her to Scotland. There were mountains there too, perhaps more beautiful than these, but Nemat always felt she shared a deep bond with the mountains of her home—the mountains where Ma had grown up and where she said she had spent the best years of her life. Nemat had always wanted to come back to these mountains. But she had never imagined it would be like this.

The taxi drove past Kakrighat; the Kosi River flowed alongside, showing the road the way. After one more turn, the river and the road would part ways, not to meet again on the road Nemat was to take, the road to Kosi, Anirudh

Thakur's town. She suddenly felt sick, her hands tightened on the purse in her lap, the words on Ma's letter came alive again.

My dear Nemat,
That you are reading this letter now means that I am gone. What you think of me after you read this letter won't matter to me now. But Nemat, my darling, I ask that you read this letter not as a daughter, but as a woman. What you think of me after reading it will be the memory of me you will always carry. Be very care—

The taxi jolted to a stop. The pages of the letter seemed to scatter with the wind that blew in through the open window. Nemat looked out, startled. A truck had suddenly appeared in front of the taxi. The taxi driver reversed a bit to let the truck pass. Nemat saw a milestone with Kosi written on it. It was either 15 or 25 kilometres. All she could read was the 5. Someone had scratched the first number out with a stone. She could have asked the taxi driver how much farther it was, but she didn't. Why had she come all this way? To meet whom? A person she hadn't even heard of until a few weeks ago. How terrible her fate was, to have to ask for help from a person she hated. From Anirudh Thakur, her mother's lover.

Anirudh Thakur, the name that had created a storm in Nemat's life when the lawyer had passed on her mother's letter along with the will. *Please try and understand my relationship with Anirudh*, her mother had written. How?

Why? The last two weeks had seen her climb many mountains, mountains of rage and disgust, of hatred and helplessness. She couldn't hate her mother and she couldn't find it in herself to forgive her. Maybe that's why she had come all this way. To decide whether she would love Ma or hate her for the rest of her life.

She saw him outside his house, pruning roses. It took every bit of courage to bring herself to speak.

'Anirudh Thakur?'

'Yes?' he turned around, surprised. He must have been between forty-five and fifty years old but his face was aglow; it was the kind of glow that only a certain peace can lend to a person. His hair was greying but he made no attempt to hide it. One shirtsleeve was rolled up to the elbow, the other was open. His hands were covered with mud. There was some mud on his kurta as well. A grey shawl was thrown loosely across his shoulders. The pureness in his honey-coloured eyes made Nemat forget for a moment how much she hated him. Ma's letter rang in her ears again.

Do you remember Loch Ness, Nemat? How transfixed you were with its water? You could sit at the edge and see all the way to the bottom. 'How can anything be this pure, Ma?' you had asked. But some things are just this pure.

I'm not saying it because I love him, but Anirudh is as pure as that water. You can look into his heart through his eyes. I know he will take care of you just the way I did.

'How can I help you, beta?' his voice jerked Nemat back to the present. Once again the hatred reared its head, but controlling herself with some effort, she said, 'I've come from Edinburgh.'

'OK,' he said, frowning slightly, trying to place her. Nemat took a deep breath and the words came out in a rush.

'Sadhika Rawat. I'm her daughter. She's dead. She said if anything happened to her I was to come to you.'

The colour drained from his face. He seemed to stagger and Nemat watched as he reached out and clutched the railing for support. He said nothing but his face, as he looked at her, showed her a man who seemed to have lost everything. She was taken aback. Did this man still love her mother? After all these years?

Still clinging to the railing, Anirudh tried to say something, but the words were stuck in his throat.

'Sorry!' His voice was hollow, as if it came from deep inside a well. He stumbled again, and Nemat stretched a hand out to help him but then drew it back. He controlled himself. Just like she had when she had seen her mother's body laid out in front of her. She realized that she hadn't wept since Ma had died. First because of shock, then disbelief, and when she had finally accepted that Ma was gone there had been no shoulder to cry on. Her parents had divorced when she was two. And her father had died a few years ago. His family had disowned Nemat and her mother even before the divorce. The man responsible for her being alone in the world was standing in front of her and she wanted to shake him like a rag doll and ask him what right he and her mother had to destroy so many lives.

'You must be tired. Come inside,' Anirudh's voice broke into Nemat's thoughts. He picked up her bags and walked in slowly, using the wall for support. She didn't want to enter his house, but something in the way he spoke made her follow him in.

As she entered the drawing room, Nemat felt that it wasn't the first time she was visiting this house. Ma had described Laxmi Vilas to her so many times that she knew every nook and corner of the place. The steps that led to the large wooden gallery, Nanaji's room at the far end and then the puja room and finally Ma's room, with an adjoining balcony suspended over a cliff with the help of a few beams. This was Ma's favourite place in the world.

This room had been Ma's room since Nemat was a little girl until after her marriage. Eventually, Nanaji had had to sell the house. The person who bought it was Anirudh Thakur.

He took Nemat's luggage into that same room.

'But this is your room!' the words were out before she could stop them.

'This room has always been Sadhika's. I simply used it. You sleep here. I'll shift to another room,' Anirudh said as he walked out the door. He had barely closed the door when he came back again and asked hesitantly, 'Is your name Nemat?'

'How do you know?' Nemat was shocked. Ma had written in her letter that she had left here before Nemat was born and that she had had no contact with Anirudh since then.

'Hmm.' Anirudh smiled wistfully and placed a gentle hand on her head. Then he left her in her room. Her hatred for this man was already starting to weaken.

Nemat looked around the room that had once been her mother's: the bed with the peacock feather design, the carved wooded shelf on the wall and big stained-glass windows. Time seemed to have stopped here. She opened the large window and stepped out on to the balcony. The evening was deepening as the clouds grew heavy and settled over the valleys. She stood on the little wooden platform, suspended above the world. Still a part of it but somehow out of its reach. Ma was right. There was a strange peacefulness in this place. Maybe that's why Anirudh had chosen this room for himself after buying the house from Nanaji. Nemat looked around herself. She seemed to have travelled nineteen years back in time. She saw Ma, hesitant, standing in front of the easy chair in the corner and Anirudh standing in front of her, a little uncertain. Ma wore a simple yellow sari and a gold chain around her neck, a thin line of vermilion filled the parting in her hair. She was a little emotional.

'I'm so sorry,' she was saying. 'I just wanted to see this room for the last time. Whenever I've been happy or sad or alone, I've always come here. It's the only place that seemed to be mine.'

'There's no need to say sorry! You can come here whenever you want. In any case, I'm mostly out on work. You won't be disturbed,' Anirudh had replied. A complete stranger had understood her so well that day. Ma didn't know then that one day she would fall in love with this stranger. She had written in her letter . . .

> Sometimes I wonder if someone else had bought that house, and if Anirudh had not taken that small storeroom of a room that was mine for his own, would my life have been different? Perhaps it would have. I would have had a family, relatives, and instead of censure I would have had respect. Sadhika Rawat, daughter of Shri Virendra Rawat, or Mrs Sadhika Harish Thakur. Yes, my life would have been different, but I wouldn't have been me.

Nemat took a deep breath. So this was the place where Ma and Anirudh's love story had started. It felt a bit strange to be standing here, but somehow it didn't fill her with as much disgust as she had felt earlier.

Night had fallen. Nemat hadn't stepped out of the room since she had arrived. Her mind was full of a strange confusion. A knock on the door startled her.

'Yes?' she said.

'Nemat, come for dinner, beta,' Anirudh said from behind the door. When Nemat went out he was sitting at the dining table. His eyes were swollen; he had been crying. As he served her khichri, he said, 'I didn't want to disturb you so I just cooked this without asking about your preferences. Sadhika really liked khichri, so I thought maybe . . .' His voice trailed away.

Nemat smiled weakly and began to eat. He had served himself but was yet to start eating.

'Who else is there in your home? I mean your wife, children?' Nemat asked.

'I never married,' Anirudh replied.

The room fell silent. The only sound was the scraping of Nemat's spoon against her plate.

That night as she sat on the balcony, Nemat took out Ma's letter again. Since Ma's death Nemat had lost count of how many times she had read the letter. But today, for the first time perhaps, she managed to read it the way Ma had wanted her to, not as her daughter, but as a woman.

It's been nineteen years since I last met Anirudh. I was expecting you. He had suggested I call you Nemat. We didn't want our relationship to harm you in any way. I never lied to your father, Nemat. I told him about my feelings for Anirudh even before I told Anirudh himself. He was a good man, your father. He accepted me even without my heart. He didn't want the world to know about what had happened. When you were about two years old, one day I saw him staring at you intently. 'Her eyes are like Anirudh's, aren't they?' he had said. That was the first time I felt that I had done something wrong. My soul was linked with Anirudh's, but even your father had been unable to get him out of his mind. I didn't want him to live with that pain. That was when I separated from him.

Think about it, Nemat. Sometimes we are handed relationships that we are expected to fulfil forever, relationships that were someone else's choice. Sometimes we do manage to fulfil them. But Anirudh was *my* choice. The only thing I don't regret in this life is my love for him.

As she continued to read, Nemat felt as if she were meeting a new Ma. The letter went on.

Illicit affair, that's what people called our relationship. But if it was, why did it never feel like I was doing anything wrong? Why did it feel so right? Why did it give me so much comfort? You know how the warm sun feels so comforting on a winter day. Anirudh was that warm sun for me, when we were together and even now when it has been so many years since I last saw him. You had asked me once if your father had loved me. Yes, he did, as much as a husband loves a wife.

Many men love a woman in her lifetime, Nemat, as a father, a brother, a friend, a husband or a son. But a woman searches for someone who understands her mind. My search ended with Anirudh.

I hope you won't hate me for what is the biggest accomplishment of my life.

Love,
Ma

Nemat didn't know how long she had been sitting there. The letter fluttered in her hands, her tears smudging the words as they fell. She didn't realize that Anirudh had come into the room and was standing behind her. He put his hand on her shoulder and sat down beside her. She tried to wipe away her tears.

'Sadhika wouldn't want us to be weak, she wouldn't like it. She didn't like crying,' Anirudh said gently. Nemat folded the letter and put it away. Two weeks ago she hadn't even heard of this man. And when she had, she'd hated him. But now she didn't feel so hateful. Perhaps she was beginning to understand their love.

'Her life was so complicated, but I never saw Ma sad. Why is that?' she asked.

Anirudh smiled. 'Was it complicated?' he asked. 'It wasn't all that much. She went wherever she wanted, and did whatever she wanted to do. There are some flowers that don't want to grow in gardens, so sensitive that if you don't touch them with tenderness they will scatter. But if you let them be, they will bloom even among rocks. That's what your mother was: a wildflower. The universe's favourite creation.' He was looking at Ma's empty armchair, as if watching his Sadhika sitting there as he spoke. Nemat looked at the empty chair and then at Anirudh. His face reflected the same peace Ma had written about in her letter. Nemat had no more questions, no more troubles. She rested her head on Anirudh's shoulder. It felt as if Ma had come back to her.

YELLOW ROSES

Jamshed Qamar Siddiqui

Sometimes, when you visit a town after a really long time, every nook and corner of its now-changed face tells you a familiar story. I was back in Shimla after seven years. The weather was beautiful. It had just stopped raining and it was slightly chilly on the Mall Road. I noticed little tea and momo stalls on either side of the road, bustling with customers. It had never been this crowded before. Quite a lot had changed. This was the town where I was born, where I made my childhood friends, where I found myself and lost myself in love. I had moved to Delhi with my job. Where had these last seven years gone?

Isn't it strange how so much happens to us every day in our busy city lives and yet we have nothing to say about it? That day, I had nothing to tell my old town except that I had changed as much as it had.

I looked at a shop right across from me, a flower shop, illuminated by the light of a single bulb. Above it a rusted board read 'Om Florist'. It was amazing, the shop was exactly the same. Outside the shop, decorated with the bouquets of gladioli and lilies and tulips, was a small tin shed, dimly lit by a bulb hanging in a holder. Exactly how it had always been. This might be the only place in the town that time hadn't changed.

This was the shop where once I used to buy yellow roses every day, yellow roses for Vishakha. Vishakha? One of those stories that this town had given me. This was where I had seen her for the first time, where I had fallen in love with her.

The flower shop was pulling me back into my past and I could remember that morning when I first saw Vishakha.

It was very cold that day, and we had counselling sessions for engineering college. I was wearing my maroon round-neck sweater. In college, students were waiting their turn outside the room where the counselling was going on. Everyone looked nervous, except one girl. She stood out in the crowd, quiet and still. She was calm, no nervous ness, no fumbling. She wore a yellow cardigan and there was a confidence on her face as she sat in the corner writing something in the last pages of her diary.

There was something about her, something that made her different from the rest of us. 'Vishakha Somvanshi!' a voice called from inside the room and she went in.

I decided right then that after the admissions process was over, I would extend a hand of friendship to Vishakha. Sometimes the effect of our wishes is so strong that God himself thinks, *Okay, let's do this and see what happens.*

My wish was granted and Vishakha and I got admission in the same college.

To tell you the truth, it was easier to be friends with Vishakha than I had anticipated. She was one of those people who took a little while to open up but once they did, they were the light of the party. We started out as members of the same group of friends but slowly, the two of us became good friends. We would often sing old songs as we ate noodles in the college canteen. We would choose old songs that were bound to make our friends laugh. Especially when we sang 'Ramaiyya Vastavaiyya', even Khan Chacha who ran the canteen would smile.

I had noticed that Vishakha had a special fascination for the colour yellow. One day as we roamed the college campus I asked her, 'What is this fascination with yellow? Yellow bag, yellow handkerchief, yellow pen, why?' 'I like it; it's the colour of friendship. That's all,' she had replied. I elbowed her as I said, 'So now in the canteen will you sing about the yellow, yellow sky?' We both laughed. She had grimaced and said, 'Bad joke number 44.'

Vishakha had a great sense of humour. In those days, unlike now, I wasn't boring and uninteresting. Maybe that's why it didn't take long for us to get really close to one another. We went from being friends to more than friends.

As we drew closer, our friends began to tease us as a couple. Vishakha didn't seem to mind at all and I would pretend to be embarrassed and they would tease us more.

The important thing about time is that be it good or bad, it passes. We didn't even know when the three years of college finished. In those three years we had become so close that we had decided that we would live and die together. We both got jobs in Shimla. On weekends we would meet at Jakhoo Hill or Anadale or sometimes the Tara Devi Temple. We would laugh a lot when we were together, often clutching our sides as we made our way home because we were laughing so hard.

I remember that afternoon on Valentine's Day. I had told her to meet me outside the Shimla State Museum. I was wearing the striped muffler she had gifted me earlier. As she approached me I held out a bouquet of yellow roses and said, 'Happy Valentine's Day, Vishakha; will you marry me?' 'Have you taken a look in the mirror?' she asked archly. 'Why?' I asked. 'You don't want to marry a good-looking guy?' We both laughed. The sun was shining on the mountains in front of us as we held hands and set off on a journey that wasn't going to be as easy as it seemed.

Often in life while we are winning a certain battle, we are losing others. My parents hadn't been so taken with Vishakha and her family but they knew love. They had had a love marriage in their day. Babuji was the accountant in the college that Ma taught at. They understood love and they understood how we felt. Despite their reservations, they began preparations for the wedding with fervour and fanfare. Both houses were busy and full of hustle-bustle and finally, on the 27th of September that very year, in the beautiful mountains of Shimla we were married.

'The wedding is complete, you are now husband and wife.' With these words from the priest we were bound together in marriage. We were happy, very happy. We felt we were touching new limits of happiness; we didn't know then that life was going to throw at us all sorts of new challenges. In those days we felt as if the spreading valleys and the endless sky were all a part of our happiness. We travelled a lot. We fought and made up. We teased each other. When I was upset she would sing funny songs to make me laugh and when she was angry I would bring her yellow roses to make her happy. We were best friends. Then, I don't know if we got busy, or if it was the decision of time, but something began to change between us.

Three months after the wedding, Vishakha got a job in a bigger company. She became an assistant manager. Her responsibilities increased and she became immersed in her work.

It was time for the Annual Conclave in her office, and she was working day and night. She would leave before I awoke and come back very late every night.

Once when she was particularly late coming home I said angrily, 'Where were you for so long? You could have called at least!' She hadn't answered and had gone swiftly to the bedroom instead. She hadn't liked the way I had spoken and the anger was the reason behind her silence that had come between us for a few days.

We had gone from being strangers to friends, and from friends to lovers, and from lovers to husband and wife. Many people climb these same steps in their relationships without realizing that as you take each new step, the previous step disappears. When Vishakha and I became friends, we weren't strangers any more, and when we became lovers, we were no longer friends, and when we got married we stopped being lovers.

'I'm sorry, Vishakha,' I messaged Vishakha a few days later. The silence was annoying me. But I got no reply from her and my anger began to grow. I was angry but I wanted this fight to stop.

When she came back I handed her a bouquet. But this time I wanted to prove my right over her. I wanted to be her husband more than her friend. This time the bouquet had red roses.

As time went by it wasn't only the colour of flowers that changed. My relationship with Vishakha changed a little every day. Every day we became more and more like a husband and wife and less and less like friends.

'What's going on in office?' I asked one Sunday as she held out a cup of tea for me, 'How is your project going?' She replied very seriously, 'It's 75 per cent done. If everything goes well hopefully it should finish before time. Oh and don't forget to take out the laundry bill today.' She picked up a newspaper from the table and began to read it.

At that moment I realized how serious our conversations had become. We had lost the mischief, the talking for no reason. And in their place we had laundry bills, ration lists and other seemingly important things.

Sometimes when I looked at her at the dinner table, as we ate in silence, I would wonder if she was the same girl with the yellow handbag who could talk about nothing for hours. The same girl who hugged me and said 'I love you' to me every morning before getting out of bed and every night before we slept. It had been an age since she had said anything like that to me.

One night while we ate she asked casually as she passed me the salad, 'So how is your job going?' 'Fine,' I replied disinterestedly and then asked, 'And yours?' 'Hmm, last minutes now . . . Oh, yes! I might have to go to Chennai next week for the project submission.'

I didn't say anything to her or even look at her. I was upset that she wasn't going to be home the next week, because it was my birthday on the fifth.

As I lay in bed that night I thought to myself that I had heard of people changing, but never an instance of anyone changing the way Vishakha had. She used to start preparing for my birthday a week in advance. She would send me gifts, record songs and what not. She would do so much to make me feel special . . . And now? She was not even going to be around on my birthday.

I wasn't interested in birthday celebrations but I was hurt by the changes in Vishakha. Many small things were now becoming issues and settling in my mind.

One afternoon I felt feverish at work. I was shivering. I took a cab and went home. I wanted to message Vishakha and tell her to come home but then I didn't. I thought she'd come home soon anyway. I waited a long time but she didn't and then at nine o'clock I got a message saying, 'Sorry! Will be late tonight.'

That night was the darkest, loneliest night of my life. I realized how deeply one can sink into loneliness. I only felt anger towards Vishakha. I thought of my mother. Even though I wasn't up to it, I got up and wrote a note to Vishakha and left it on the table. And then, trembling as I drove, I went to my parents. That sad moment had decided that Vishakha didn't need me and I didn't need her.

After driving for a few hours I reached home. I had taken leave from office for a week and come home to my parents. 'You did a good thing by coming home,' Ma said as she applied a cold compress to my forehead. I had told them that Vishakha was busy and that's why I had come home. They believed me.

The next morning, there were eighteen missed calls from Vishakha on my phone and some messages apologizing and asking me to come home. I remembered the time when we used to roam carefree on the restless roads. Who would have thought our journey together would be so short?

The next evening, as I stood on the balcony watching children play cricket I felt a hand on my shoulder. It was Ma.

'What's wrong, what's happened? Tell me,' she said. I answered hurriedly, 'Nothing, nothing has happened. Why should anything happen? I was missing you both so I came home.' She smiled and said, 'Say what you will, your face is saying something else. Something is wrong. Now tell me. Come on.'

Tears welled up in my eyes. You can hide things from yourself, but not from your mother. I told her everything, from beginning to end. I only looked at her after I had finished.

She was smiling. I was shocked! 'That's all?' she asked.

Gesturing to me to sit on the chair near her she said, 'Your generation is very confused about love. Actually you learn about love from movies, where every scene is full of action. Maybe that's why you think that there is love only if something is going on all the time, fighting, singing, joking. Isn't it?'

It was as if Ma's words had opened a skylight in my mind. I found a new way to think. She told me how everything changes with time, even the ways in which we show love. Our behaviour, the way we talk, maybe we hesitate to show love. But that doesn't mean there is no love. It just means there is no noise in love, there is deepness. That night Ma's words were like hammer blows in my head. The next morning I watched Ma and Babuji sitting on a cot in the garden. Ma was reading the paper and Babuji was shelling peas. They weren't talking, but they were connected, there was love—the same love as when they had got married. I thought they mustn't have always been like this; they must have laughed and teased each other once. The expression of their love may have changed but it was still love, wasn't it?

Maybe I was worrying about the changes in Vishakha needlessly? Maybe our relationship was deepening and not becoming lifeless as I was imagining? I had found my answers. We had drifted apart because our friendship had drifted. I had become just a husband. Earlier, if she had been out late I would have been worried, not angry. If she had had too much work I would have helped her, not criticized her. I realized neither of us was wrong. Only time had changed. Something was breaking inside my mind.

'Ma! I'm leaving,' I said. 'I'll come again next week.' They both smiled as I left; they knew I had understood.

I wept on the drive back at the way I had treated her. I berated myself. I knew she would have left for Chennai but I wanted to reach home, call her from the landline and say, 'I've come home. Please forgive me.' I was angry with myself.

But there was a surprise waiting for me at home. The door wasn't locked. When I went in, Vishakha was there. She looked at me with shocked, tear-filled eyes. Before she could say anything I said, 'I'm sorry, Vishakha.'

In the way that the longest journeys start with the smallest step, sometimes the smallest step can bridge the widest distances. I had taken that step and as we held each close we knew that no misunderstanding could drive a wedge between us.

We realized that we both had complaints against each other. We both had looked at things from only our individual perspectives. I discovered that Vishakha had lied about going to Chennai; she had been planning a surprise for my birthday. We still had place for mischief, just of a different kind.

We had never held each other with the desperation with which we clung to each other that day. Our heartbeats became one. 'Vishakha, I can't promise to become a good husband, but I promise you that I will always remain a good friend.'

Everything became all right after that. That evening, as we ate momos at a small stall along Mall Road, Vishakha held a bouquet of yellow roses.

Since then I always gifted her a bouquet of yellow roses from that shop on every special occasion. She was a strange girl—the most expensive gift in the world couldn't light up her eyes the way those yellow roses could.

After being in Shimla for many years we both moved to Delhi. She is still crazy about yellow roses. We may not drum tables and sing 'Ramaiyya Vastavaiyya' any more, or laugh like crazy, but our love is just the way it was.

Look at the time! I better stop and pick up some roses before the shop closes.

LETTERS

Anulata Raj Nair

The house was strewn with the things unloaded from the truck. It was quite a job unpacking things that had been packed by the packers. Huge wooden crates and cardboard boxes swathed in tape lay everywhere. There was a strange smell in the house. The house didn't look like home. Nothing was familiar; there was no fragrance of belonging.

I was trying to put my things in order. Tanvi had gone to sleep, tired. I was tired too, but I didn't want to sleep without putting away the papers that lay scattered around the room. At least there was the satisfaction of knowing that this would be the last shift. After thirty-five years of government service, I had finally retired at the age of sixty. No more transfers, and no more packing and unpacking.

I had emptied the contents of two steel trunks on to the floor in the hope that things might get sorted out and thrown away.

I was wiping the bundles of paper with a duster before putting them away, unread. I knew they weren't useful, not really. They were just some old letters which I had put away by force of habit.

It was then that I saw, peeping out from among the papers, a light pink ribbon. I held a corner and pulled.

Suddenly the wall that separated my past and my present crumbled and fell away. In a second, I had travelled forty years back in time—to the day when the envelope with the pink ribbon had first been in my hand. The postman had been smiling as he had handed me the letter, as if he had understood its contents.

The pale pink of the envelope had tempted me to smell it to see if it had any fragrance. And it had. The faint heady scent of roses.

I had hid the letter behind my back immediately because Babuji had heard the postman and had come outside. Timed exactly like the entry of the villain!

Now forty years later, I held the letter up to my face and inhaled deeply, but the fragrance was gone.

For some reason my hands shook like those of a man newly in love. I wanted to read those words again as soon as I could. The words I had never been able to forget.

He said she had gone to sleep and I hid the letter behind my back like I had done all those years ago.

My heart was beating fast.

Tanvi and I were happy by all accounts. We were a sensible and sorted couple. It was a different matter that I had hidden the complications of my heart from her for thirty years. Sometimes it had seemed to me as if Tanvi was peering inside my mind, trying to see what I was hiding. But maybe I had imagined it.

I was thirty when we got married and Tanvi twenty-five. I was a bit old for marriage by the standards of the day. It's obvious that it was the contents of that pink envelope that were linked to the delay.

'What happened?' Tanvi's voice surprised me.

I hid the pink envelope which was still behind my back in the pages of the autobiography I was writing.

What a strange dichotomy! This love story from my past was now hiding in my autobiography in which I had been deceitful in not mentioning it at all.

Maybe I had been deceitful with our relationship as well.

My heart beat fast, like a teenager stepping into the shining world of love for the first time, and whose first love letter had been caught.

An old story, a feeling from long ago, had come and snatched away my peace. Maybe this was the essence of love. No matter how much you suppress it, bury it six feet under the ground, it breathes.

What was happening to me now? And at the age of sixty!

'What's happened to you?' Tanvi asked again and I was pulled back into the present.

Troubled, she came and sat down next to me.

'What's happened? Are you well?' She rubbed my chest and began to rummage through the medicine box to find my blood pressure medicine.

I pulled myself together and drank a glass of cold water. I felt a bit better.

Then I looked at Tanvi and smiled—an empty, hollow smile. I wanted to convince her that I was well so that she would go back to sleep and I could read once again, after forty years, that pink letter whose fragrance was still fresh in my consciousness. And remember all those things that I had promised to forget . . .

The wall clock struck twelve. Like the pendulum striking the hour I too was swinging between the past and the present.

I didn't sleep that night.

That day kept coming alive, the day I was the eighteen-year-old boy who had been handed that scented pink envelope.

It was during the seventies when people used to write letters to stay in touch. Writing and reading letters played a very important part in people's lives then; it did in mine, at least.

Maybe that was why I had saved all those letters for so many years: Babuji's letters filled with advice, Ma's sad letters, my sister's rakhi letters filled with love, some letters from relatives and also some pink envelopes that held fragrant letters.

These letters were my treasure.

Sometimes in a childish attempt to relive the old days I still write letters to Ma and some old friends.

It was strange that I had never written to Tanvi. Maybe those pink letters had left a thorn in my heart and that was why I had never told Tanvi about them. Tanvi had never complained and I had convinced myself that she had no interest in writing or receiving letters. I had saved myself with ease.

In the days of letter writing, having penfriends was a big craze. The weekly magazine that we subscribed to had a list of names and addresses on the last page that intrigued me and urged me to write to someone. I was hesitant to be the first to write but I had sent my name and address in a few issues.

Maybe it was destined that love would hit me through a rose pink envelope and one day I got that first scented letter.

Apart from my name that letter had just two lines:

Dear Vijay,
I am a sixteen-year-old girl. I can't promise that I will prove to be a good friend. Reply if you feel like.

Anamika

For some reason I took that letter as a challenge and I wrote back the same day. On a plain inland form were two lines:

Dear Anamika,
I am sure we will be really good friends.
Write soon.

Vijay

That was the first letter I ever wrote to a girl. My first love letter.

I remember writing my entire biodata to Anamika in the very next letter: where I lived, what I did, how I loved reading and intended to publish my autobiography one day, that I loved watching films and that I had a heart full of love. And of course my height, the colour of my skin, how I looked, everything, I wrote everything in that second letter.

Actually, it was a clever ruse on my part, for I received everything that I wanted to know about her in her reply: what she liked doing, how she looked, what she thought, what she wanted from life.

I was well aware of the fact that the same person who had written everything about himself in that second letter to a girl he had never met had spent a whole lifetime hiding his past from his wife, while quietly keeping it alive all this time.

And it's sad, because Tanvi had always felt that I didn't love her deeply, she always felt that something was missing, incomplete. I always stubbornly denied the truth.

The story of letters between me and Anamika took off.

At first, we wrote formally but slowly we began to share our deepest feelings. Things like, 'Today my father was very angry with me,' or 'I saw that film today, and it reminded me of you.'

And she would write, 'Today I rode on a classmate's bike. I hope you don't mind?'

We were getting closer.

I had never got as close to Tanvi in thirty years of marriage as I had to Anamika just through letters.

Coming across those letters suddenly had thrown me into great confusion. I would look at the letters and then at the pages of my almost complete autobiography. Tanvi had helped me so much in writing it—technical help, like drafting, proofreading, etc.

But after finding that letter I felt that I had left a beautiful part of my life out of my autobiography. That was a huge travesty. Against myself.

So I decided to add a few more pages to my story.

But the problem was, what would I say to Tanvi and how?

Whenever I got the chance I would take Anamika's letters out and read every line over and over again.

They were filled with love, filled with the fragrance of the earth after the first rain, the bittersweet taste of young love.

I looked for the last letter she wrote to me, the letter that had changed my life. I remembered all those bitter words, words that altered my taste for life.

After a year and half of pure love-filled letters she had written:

> This was all a joke for me, a way of passing the time. I don't love you and my name is not Anamika; it is Saroj. Don't write to me any more. My address has changed.
> Goodbye.

That letter had shaken me deeply. Over the past year and a half I had done nothing else except love Anamika. But I had worked hard to win her over and earn her appreciation, and get admission in a good engineering college.

I didn't get Anamika but I did get admission into a good college, and if I put aside love, everything improved in my life after that.

And I *had* put love aside, but suddenly, after all these years, the feeling was awakening. The emotions that had been sidelined all these years were now suddenly flowing out.

I knew I wanted to include my one and only love story in my autobiography—as if to make a dishonest relationship honest, legitimate. But did I have the courage to accept that I hadn't loved my wife as much as I loved Anamika? And would Tanvi be able to endure this truth?

'Now what? You want to change something again?' she grumbled as she came and sat close to me. 'At this rate this book will never get published.'

'Tell me. What needs to be removed or added?' she looked intently at me trying to read my expression.

Wordlessly I handed her a letter from Anamika.

She read it and smiled.

'You were eighteen then, right?'

'Hmm,' I nodded.

'Are there more letters?' she asked.

I looked deep in her eyes. Tanvi was calm, as she always was.

Reluctantly I handed her the whole bundle of letters.

She read them all. Then she said softly, 'I think her name was Anamika and none of this was a joke.'

'Why do you say that?' I asked quietly.

Wiping the corner of her eyes with the corner of her sari she said, 'I'm a woman, I can understand her.'

I tried to read Tanvi's mind. I felt relieved after having told Tanvi about Anamika; lighter, like some weight had been lifted from me. Eventually I did write about Anamika in my autobiography. I wrote about our letters but I didn't know what to call our relationship. Was it love? What was the truth? How should I write about those untouched moments? I was confused. As always Tanvi came to the rescue. We called it an unfinished love story.

There were some things from those letters which I couldn't bring myself to write about, like the time she had written that she slept with my letters under her pillow. Just that thought had kept me awake for so many nights.

I was happy that I had written almost everything about my life truthfully in my book. I was happy that Tanvi had understood me so well, that she hadn't condemned me for it. For the first time I felt in love with Tanvi.

My book was published. I got some fan mail and a few phone calls. I felt satisfied that my book was a success.

Some day later a pink envelope came in the post. The handwriting was familiar. My heart raced. With shaking hands I lifted the letter to my face and breathed deeply. I laughed at my childishness!

There was a small letter inside.

Dear Vijay,
So you finally wrote your autobiography, and so truthfully! Congratulations!

In response to your honesty, I want to share something with you. I didn't write that last letter

to you myself. My father made me write it so that I
would not have any trouble getting married because
of you.

My name is Anamika, not Saroj.

And that was not a joke, I did love you.

Anamika

Just then the door opened and Tanvi entered.

Once again I was hiding a letter behind my back,
trembling like a pipal leaf. There was a strange silence in
the room.

Silently I handed the letter to Tanvi.

I had understood the hurt of an incomplete and
dishonest love. That hurt had now healed.

Tanvi was looking at me surprised. There was nothing
except love and trust in her eyes. I went to her and held her
hand. Her fingers closed tightly around mine.

The fragrance from the flowers in her hair filled
the room.

SATRANGI

Manjit Thakur

The old mansion stood defiantly at the farthest end of the small town of Madhupur. Hastings House it was called. The only broken-down road that entered Madhupur stopped abruptly when it encountered the jungle that used to be the garden of Hastings House. The once grand garden was now overgrown and wild.

The mansion was dilapidated and desperately in need of repair. No one ventured near it. Not even the cowherds. There were a couple of graves in the grounds of Hastings House and the town's people believed that a ghost from one of those graves haunted the mansion.

Hastings House had once belonged to an Englishman but now Bauji was the owner. Bauji was one of the bigger zamindars of the area and lived in the city. Then some of the villagers, influenced by communists, had taken over the land amidst slogans of he who shall till the land shall own the land. Bauji had had to come back to Madhupur to save his lands.

With Bauji came his son, Chandramohan, and his daughter, Vibha. Though Vibha was married she didn't get along with her husband and so she stayed with her father and cursed her husband and in-laws, swearing that she would only eat properly and sleep peacefully after she saw them dead.

Before Bauji and his family moved back the house had been repaired properly. Some cracks remained despite all efforts and the inhabitants lived with God's name on their lips. Then during the summer wedding season Chandramohan got married to a girl called Satrangi. Unlike Chandramohan in every way, she was fair and beautiful and well-spoken. There was no comparison. Chandramohan had small eyes, hers were big and kohl-lined. His nose was bulbous, hers was sharp. With her graceful neck and waist-length hair she looked like a fairy.

Chandramohan was uneducated and Satrangi had topped the whole district in the Class Twelve examinations. She wrote poetry and stories, and everyone had known that she would make something of her life.

But then sometimes a twist comes along and something unexpected happens. At Satrangi's mother's insistence, Satrangi's father who was a very influential person, denied her permission to do anything else with her life and married her off immediately.

It was their wedding night. Satrangi waited for Chandramohan.

Chandramohan came home in a drunken stupor, his eyes red. He lifted her veil and she looked away coyly. All the girls in college had talked about how the groom would be tall, dark and handsome. But the reek of alcohol in his breath was unbearable for Satrangi. After walking around uneasily for a while, Chandramohan went to the bathroom to vomit, and Satrangi sat on the bed waiting for him, her chin resting on her drawn-up knees, when suddenly she saw a shadow near the window.

She was terrified and lay down pretending to be asleep. She wanted to make believe she hadn't seen anything. Exhausted after a long day, Satrangi did finally fall asleep. But all the while, somewhere at the back of her mind, the feeling lingered that there was someone else in her room.

It was true that there had been shadow there. The shadow had stood there, terrified, the whole night. He had lived in that mansion for two hundred years. Usually he never left the mansion after sunrise. He was the reason no one ventured near the place, even when it had been empty.

The shadow stood still against the wall. He was scared. The shadow, who the world called a ghost, was terrified of humans. Ghosts have fewer emotions than people. If there is love in people there is also hate, and hatred can cause a lot of pain.

The shadow saw the new bride emerge from the bathroom after her bath, her hair still damp. He watched Satrangi water the sacred Tulsi plant and light the oil lamp. Then she climbed the stairs up to her room. He was cautious now as he watched her.

There was a strange perfume in Satrangi's freshly washed hair which had dampened the edge of her sari. He drew close to her. Very close. He knew she wouldn't be able to see him unless he wanted her to.

Satrangi looked shyly at her reflection in the mirror as she combed her hair. She had forgotten that the previous night had been her wedding night, her first night with her husband. But even she couldn't remember when her drunk husband had finished vomiting and had come and passed out on the bed.

She felt sad. Her dreams had already begun to die. She was so full of potential, and her husband . . . ?

For Satrangi her husband was nothing more than a limp drunkard. Her deep eyes filled with tears. As she applied kajal to her moist eyes the shadow drew even closer. He wanted to look deep into her eyes.

She opened her eyes wide to apply the kajal, her eyeballs moving from right to left, and he thought she looked like a fish. The shadow moved even closer to those eyes and suddenly Satrangi felt warm breath on her face.

It was a familiar smell. 'Who is it?' she asked, uncertain.

The shadow couldn't control himself; he drew close to her and whispered in her ear, 'It's me, Robert Clive.'

'Clive? Clive who?'

'A ghost. The ghost of this mansion.'

Satrangi wasn't scared. She was strangely excited. And filled with this excitement she went about her daily tasks. She always felt as if someone was walking alongside her. In the kitchen, in the granary, in the courtyard, wherever she went, she always felt Robert near her.

At first she found the thought of a shadow being attached to her in the loneliness of the crowded house a bit unpleasant. But she also felt alone whenever Robert wasn't around.

One night she was pleasantly surprised. She had just emerged from her bath and flowers began to appear on her wet footprints—oleander on the first, jasmine on the second and hibiscus on the third. Robert Clive . . . Satrangi smiled.

Days grew into weeks, and weeks into months.

Satrangi was no longer a new bride. She had been the darling in her home, but here in her husband's house everyone put her down. Vibha seemed to have left her own husband's house only to dance on Satrangi's head. Trying her best to ignore Vibha's taunts and sneers Satrangi cooked, cleaned the rice, washed and dried wheat, and if there was still time left she would make cow-dung pats for the fire.

Chandramohan would leave for the fields at the crack of dawn and would return for lunch. Before Satrangi could even speak him properly he would pick up his motorbike and leave for the nearby market. But when Satrangi finished all her chores and returned to her room, her mind was refreshed. Sometimes she would find bunches of jasmine on her bed, or the foot of the bed would be covered with a pillow of flowers.

Outside her room, as far as her in-laws were concerned, Satrangi was nothing more than a maidservant. Make tea for Bauji, or Chandramohan's favourite mutton biryani, or oil Vibha's hair and remove the nits.

But Robert always treated her like a queen. When she returned tired to her room he would take the jar of oil from her cupboard and would massage her beautiful, soft feet.

The coconut oil would smell of jasmine and the bath water in the bucket of rose water. At night she would go up on to the roof and he would sit like her shadow at her feet and tell her stories that were 200 years old.

One day while she was kneading dough, a strand of her hair fell across her face and Robert gently blew it away. He enjoyed that so much that he would often blow gently at her face.

Satrangi laughed, 'How come you're so sweet, Robert?'

She didn't notice that Vibha had heard her laughing and was watching as she seemingly talked to herself.

The next day was a very difficult one for Satrangi. Vibha had the whole household worked up. 'Bhabhi is mad, she talks to herself. On moonlit nights she recites poems to the wind.'

Soon the whole of Madhupur knew that the zamindar's daughter-in-law was going mad. Before Bauji could come to know of it, Satrangi had been locked up inside her room. Instead of making her sad and lonely, Satrangi was relieved. She was free of her drunkard husband and that courtyard. Robert was always around her. 'Satrangi! Satrangi!' he would call out to her.

Satrangi had fallen in love with Robert Clive's voice. He had a treasure trove of stories: incidents about the Madhupur area, the deaths from malaria and black fever, how the area used to be called Kalapani, meaning black water, and many other stories of lakes full of fish and fields full of rice.

Robert had drawn near Satrangi one day and whispered in her ear, 'If I had been alive I would never had let your feet touch the ground. I would have put my palms under them for you to walk on.'

Satrangi smiled. Robert's voice was deep and still. She hadn't seen him but she loved his voice.

For her Robert was his voice. She didn't like to be without him for even a moment now. Robert had shown her his grave from the window of her room and told her the story of his death. The price for his love had been his life. Neither the local people nor the East India Company had been happy with him. This was the spot where he had shot himself.

Satrangi's eyes swam with tears. 'The price of love will be death in this lifetime too,' she said.

She had been locked up in the room for a week now. Bauji still didn't know anything about it or that she had gone without food or water for all these days, that very girl who he had emotionally declared would be like his daughter when he had taken dowry from her father.

Anyway, Bauji was Bauji; for him local politics was more important than the people in his house. But Chandramohan at least should have noticed. But he knew nothing. He would go to the fields in the morning and then where he went in the evenings nobody knew. Or at least everyone in Madhupur knew but his family feigned ignorance.

Satrangi sat on her bed, broken, tired, her head resting on her knees. Two days after she had been locked up Vibha had entered the room with an exorcist and some old women from the neighbouring houses. The exorcist wore a strange Turkish hat on his head with a rainbow tassel.

As soon as he had seen her he had said that she was haunted by a ghost, and that the ghost was in love with her long hair. They had pounced on her and shorn her head and tied her up in shackles. The door was locked from outside. According to the exorcist the lock was sacred and would prevent any ghost from coming near Satrangi.

Robert had disappeared at that moment. Satrangi had wept, 'Robert! Where are you? See what they have done to me!'

There had been no answer.

But in the evening, once again the room was filled with the fragrance of flowers. She had lifted her head from her knees to see her bed strewn with flowers, hibiscus, jasmine, tuberose and Arabian jasmine. She heard Robert say, 'I went to collect them for you. Did you think that fraud of an exorcist could stop me? No one can stop love.'

She smiled through her tears. She showed him the bruises on her back. The air became damp with the scent of tears, like the breeze after it rains.

'Are you crying, Robert?' Satrangi asked.

There had been no response but she felt as though someone was caressing her bare back with flower petals. The pain eased.

The sensation had tickled her and she had laughed out loud. Her laughter rang threw Hastings House. The tinkling laughter had filled Vibha's heart with dread.

Now the disgrace of the family had spread beyond Madhupur to the areas around it. People were laughing at them. Satrangi heard that Vibha was going to poison her with kheer that night.

She heard Robert call her name, 'Satrangi!'

'Satrangi is dying. You are a ghost. What can become of a ghost and a human? I can't see you and I never will. You're just a voice . . .' Satrangi's eyes filled with tears. 'Tonight is my last night, Robert.'

There was no sound from Robert.

The door opened and Vibha and the exorcist walked in. She had a bowl of kheer in her hand.

'Here, eat this,' she said roughly.

Wordlessly Satrangi took the bowl from her and ate the kheer. Robert pleaded with her to not do this, but Satrangi covered herself with a sheet and lay down. The household got busy preparing for her death.

She had eaten the poison but was wide awake. She didn't feel drugged. There was no pain. Robert came up to her and said, 'Come to the mirror.'

She went to the mirror and there in the dim light of the lamp she saw reflected in it standing right behind her a handsome young Englishman. He wore an officer's uniform and his golden hair fell across his forehead. His eyes were blue.

She smiled. 'Now I see you, in my last hour?'

She could see Robert, and touch him. He took her hand and walked her over to the window. 'It's not the last hour, it's the beginning.'

They stepped out of the window together and glided through the air. The ground below them was dark, but up amongst the clouds white moonlight surrounded them.

They both settled on another mansion. Robert caught her hands and said, 'No humans come here and so neither does their hatred. This is the dwelling of love.'

The mansion was called Satrangi.

MUNJHI'S PALACE

Kanchan Pant

Just two bends in the road before Jaisalmer is Munjhi's Palace. Now why Munjhi calls this eight-by-six-foot square stall her palace is another story, one to be told at leisure.

It was peak tourist season in this Rajasthani town. The shops were crammed with tourists and the shopkeepers hardly had time to breathe. But not Munjhi; she was calm as she showed the couple in her shop Bandhej saris one after the other, as if she had all the time in the world.

'Here, Didi *sa*, look at this one! This particular design was a favourite of the Princess of Jodhpur. She had thousands of them.' Her eyes shone as she spoke. The woman pushed it away and said, 'This is too expensive. Show me something else.'

Munjhi opened a new bundle of saris, and as she unfurled a turquoise one she said, 'Don't worry about the price, Didi sa, just choose something you like; if you don't like the price, take it as a gift from me. One should have the heart

43

of a princess; what's the money got to do with it? Isn't that so, Jeeja sa?' she addressed the lady's husband.

The husband who had been standing despondently all this while started looking at the saris too. They had been in the shop for half an hour and had bought nothing so far. During the season most shopkeepers didn't pay much attention to this kind of shopper. But not Munjhi. Her sharp eyes caught the woman looking at the lacquer bangles. She swiftly took down some boxes and spread the contents before the woman.

'You must take some bangles with you,' she said. 'Even Rani Jodhabai's bangles always went from Jaisalmer.' The story began with bangles and went to *maangtika*s and chokers and on to glass-sequinned saris and kurtas with the quintessential *gota patti*. When half an hour later the couple left the shop, their arms were laden with packages and their faces wreathed in smiles.

No customer left Munjhi's shop empty-handed. Everyone knew that. She was proud of her palace. It was another matter that her family didn't like it all that much.

The family was large: her three maternal uncles and their wives, their children and grandchildren, and her mother— Ma. Munjhi felt pity for Ma, more than love. She didn't like the others because they didn't like her. She had only one dream: to build a two-room house behind her shop, get married and then live there in peace. Ever since she had set up this shop she had been saving money in a piggy bank she kept behind the table—money for her house. And she had already found the person she was going to live with in her palace.

It was Ganesh, the guy who worked in Chauhan Tours and Travels. Munjhi said she loved him, but people felt their relationship was defined more by fighting than loving.

'You used to be a wastrel once, a complete ass!' she would say to him. 'It's I who has taught you sense and made a man of you. You'd still be roaming around with those useless friends of yours if not for me!'

Not to be outdone, Ganesh would reply, 'Yes you are the princess of some unknown palace! Go and look after your shop. Don't irritate me!'

But if anybody made the mistake of getting involved they would both gang up against that person. 'Listen, I will say whatever has to be said to Ganesh. Who are you to speak about him?' Munjhi would say.

Munjhi didn't know anything about the love they show in movies. For her love meant that Ganesh was the only person in the world who she could fight with to her heart's content. Not that Ganesh had said anything conventional like 'I love you' to her either. A few months ago he had jokingly put some money into Munjhi's piggy bank. That was it; from that day on, it was decided that he had the rights to both the piggy bank and her heart. Even though Munjhi had decided that she would get married only after her palace was completed, she had already learnt how to order him around like a bossy wife. From yelling at his mother to taking her medicines on time to getting his younger brother Kartik to start working, Munjhi did everything better than Ganesh. Kartik was in awe of Munjhi. They were the same age and he was more likely to listen to her than to his brother. For Ganesh, his house had finally started feeling like a home.

Munjhi loved Ganesh. She never needed to hide anything from him. She didn't need to dress up for him, nor did she need to be anything else to please him. He had seen her as she was since she'd been a little girl, with a running nose, wild hair and her clothes invariably torn. Her father had died early on and it seemed her mother had forgotten about her after giving birth to her. And she never had time anyway; it was as if the world depended on her work. Munjhi would drift from place to place like a vagabond. People would yell at her, 'Go and wash you face!' or 'Chhi! Look at your hair! You look like a demon. Why don't you tell your mother to brush your hair?' or 'Don't sit on the bed with those dirty clothes.'

But her mother didn't have time to wash her face again and again or sew her torn dresses. Munjhi wasn't sad about the state of affairs in her house; it just made her obstinate and blunt. The only person to have truly loved her was Ganesh. He was a bit silly, but so what? Munjhi knew he was the only person in the world who wouldn't betray her.

It was well past lunchtime. Munjhi was hungry. Her stomach was rumbling. Her tiffin box sat in front of her but she couldn't eat. She had got so used to eating with Ganesh. He would always come to her shop during his lunch break and they would eat together. But they had had a fight this morning and Munjhi had told him never to show his face to her again.

Indeed she had said it, but she didn't mean it! This really annoyed her about Ganesh—he would believe anything anyone said. Shouldn't a man have a mind of his own? Everyone who had come near the shop since morning had heard about their quarrel, from the neighbouring shopkeepers to her customers. She was becoming a little worried now. She might fight as much as she liked but she couldn't stay without him either.

Her gaze alighted on her neighbour, Raju. 'Ay Raju!' she called out to him. Raju was on his way to play cricket, his great obsession. 'I don't have time,' he called back. 'The match is starting.'

'*Match ke bachche!* Should I tell your father where you run off to after bunking school? You better come here quietly,' Munjhi threatened. Carrying his bat like a mace on his shoulder, Raju gave in. She handed him a tiffin box from her cloth bag. 'Give this to Ganesh and, if he asks about me, tell him Munjhi is dead.' Raju picked up the tiffin box unenthusiastically; it wasn't the first time these two were fighting.

'And listen!' she called to his retreating back. 'Bring back my tiffin box. Empty. Understand?'

Raju made a face at her and ran off with the tiffin.

Half an hour had passed since Raju had left with the tiffin box. But neither the box nor Ganesh had appeared. *He must be really angry this time*, Munjhi thought and went to the shop next door. 'Kaka sa, please mind my shop for a bit. I'll just be back,' she told the shopkeeper.

When she reached Chauhan Tours and Travels, she found Ganesh sitting with his head down on the table. The unopened tiffin box lay beside him on the bench.

Loudly she said, 'Why do I bother to cook for people if they can't even appreciate it?'

When he didn't respond to her jibe or raise his head she got worried. She went up to him and, ruffling his hair, she asked, 'Are you ill? Look at me.'

When he looked up, her hands stopped in shock. Ganesh had a swollen eye and bruises on his face. He had been beaten up by someone.

Out of the two of them, Munjhi was the one who had taken on the responsibility of all fighting. Be it Thanvi Sahab who parked his scooter right in front of the door, or that Bansal who stole electricity from Ganesh's meter to run his internet cafe, or Ganesh's friend Santosh who teased him about her, Munjhi had fixed them all. At times like these Ganesh would don the role of a saint. 'Let it go, Munjhi, why fight about such a small thing?' he would say.

It was the second time this week that the same peaceable Ganesh had fought with someone.

'Who did this?' Munjhi asked as she caressed a bruise. He flinched.

'No one. I fell,' he said.

'Don't annoy me, Ganesh, tell me who did this,' Munjhi said as she applied ointment on his wounds. Ganesh looked at her. Her face was flushed with anger, her nose red. He watched her as she mumbled to herself while tending to his bruises. Normally she bullied him and ordered him around, but if he was ever ill or troubled she would start mothering him. Ganesh liked this Munjhi best.

'I had borrowed some money from someone. It got a bit ugly when they came to ask for it back. It's sorted now,' he said. Munjhi looked at him as if she would eat him alive. She was fed up of his borrowing money from here and there. Why would anyone beg for a thousand bucks? But he just didn't understand.

'Don't be angry. I said it's been arranged,' Ganesh said as he held her hand. She jerked her hand out of his clasp and stormed out of the shop.

When she returned a little later she was carrying her piggy bank. She threw it on the ground and the floor was strewn with notes and coins. 'Take what you need to pay back the loan and clear it today,' she snapped. Ganesh looked at her with amazement. He needed to say something to her but he couldn't. He wished he could just speak out like Munjhi. Munjhi said you shouldn't hide things from the person you love; you jinx your love if you do. Their love was about to be jinxed.

Something had been troubling Ganesh for a few months now. It was the reason he was getting into fights. He should have told Munjhi about it. He had the chance but he hadn't been able to say it to her. He probably wouldn't be able to say it now either.

'Are you even listening to me?' she asked. Her voice jerked him back to the present.

'You broke your bank for me? Your house?' he asked, still in shock.

'Don't overreact, Ganesh. You know I'll do anything for you.' She hit him playfully as she spoke. No, he wouldn't be able to tell Munjhi today. Whether it was true or not, either way Munjhi would kill him.

Ganesh threw the pieces of the shattered piggy bank into the bin and, pressing the notes into her hand, he said, 'Crazy girl! You keep this money for your house. I don't need it.' Munjhi looked into his eyes, searching for something. She could always tell if he was lying; when she was convinced that he meant it, she took the money and asked, 'Will you come with me to Mamool ki Medhia today?'

Smiling, Ganesh nodded. Munjhi loved the derelict palace just outside town. Legend went that Princess Mamool had killed herself in this palace when her lover Rana Mahendra Singh had doubted her. When she went there, Munjhi would mostly be silent as she contemplated the crumbling walls of the palace. This was the only time Ganesh would see her quiet.

'You do love me?' Munjhi asked him. He felt as if she had caught him out. To hide his agitation he replied, 'Do you doubt it?'

Munjhi looked at him for a moment and then asked sternly, 'If I doubted you I would kill you, wouldn't I?'

She was back to her old self. Ganesh smiled. Munjhi wanted to tell him her secret that day itself—that their two-room house was almost ready. He would be so happy. She had secretly started work on it a few months ago. Now only the floor was left to finish. She and Kartik were going to Jodhpur to get marble for it.

The day Munjhi and Kartik returned from Jodhpur, as they were unloading the small truck, they heard Santosh's voice, 'Now do you believe me? I told you they had both gone together.' Munjhi turned around in shock. Ganesh and Santosh were standing there, Ganesh with a million questions and disbelief on his face. Kartik too had turned around. Flustered, he said, 'Bhai sa, I just went to meet a client. I met Munjhi di on the way back and gave her a lift.'

'Can you hear the lies? You are a simple man but these two think you are an idiot,' Santosh stoked the fire. He had resented Munjhi ever since she had shouted at him in public. But Ganesh silenced him with a glare and he slunk back.

Munjhi was stunned. 'What nonsense is this Santosh talking?' she asked.

'It's not nonsense. Swear that there is nothing between the two of you.' Ganesh's words burned Munjhi like molten iron.

'Are you out of your mind?' Munjhi trembled with fury. She still couldn't believe that Ganesh had spoken the words that she had heard.

'If it isn't the truth, why are you afraid to swear?' The bitterness in Santosh's heart infected his words. Munjhi turned to stone. She wanted to cry but couldn't. She wanted to fight but couldn't. She wanted to berate Ganesh but couldn't. For the first time in her life, Munjhi couldn't find the words.

'I swear on Shambhuji, Bhai sa. Santosh is lying. Munjhi di, why don't you just swear?' Burning from the insult, Kartik's voice was shaking. Ganesh's heart was beating fast. If only Munjhi would swear that there was nothing between her and Kartik, everything would be all right.

It was the same town, the same doubt, the same pride. Munjhi was Mamool and Ganesh was Mahendra Singh. But unlike Mamool, this princess of today wasn't going to prove her innocence. She said, 'I won't swear.' Her voice was icy. Her face was white. Kartik's face fell at her words, Santosh smirked with revenge and victory. Ganesh and Munjhi stood facing each other. Ganesh's anger had disappeared, replaced by infinite sadness. In broken words he said, 'You repaid my love with betrayal?'

'Love?' The icy tone and her gaze made Ganesh shiver. 'If I had made a mistake and you had still forgiven me, that would have been love. Now whether I swear or not, whether this blot between us gets washed away or doesn't, there can be no love between us,' she spoke calmly and began to rummage around in her purse. She drew out some crumpled notes and put them in Ganesh's hand. 'Here is the money you put in the money box for our palace. We owe each other nothing now,' she said and, turning around, walked away towards her shop.

HOME

Anulata Raj Nair

It was still half an hour to midnight. I looked at the wall clock that showed me the time in India in addition to the local London time. It was my feeble attempt to stay connected to my country.

I was pretending to be asleep, although sleep was miles away from my eyes. No pain or trouble or worry kept me from sleeping. I was awake in anticipation. I knew that at the stroke of midnight I would hear whispering outside my door, and then an eye would peer through the keyhole followed by the sound of suppressed giggles.

And then with a loud commotion my wife and both my sons would enter my room, to celebrate my sixtieth birthday. In just a little while, my room would be filled with flowers and brightly coloured ribbons and presents. And before I knew it, sometime during the raucous singing of 'Happy Birthday', a cake would be cut and smeared on everyone's faces.

I can say all this with such certainty because this is how it has been for the last few years.

I'm lucky to have two grown-up boys and a wife who love me so much. Life with them passed so effortlessly, like flowing water caressing the soles of my feet.

The clock struck twelve.

I was surprised. How come? It was twelve. What had happened to the children today? Had they forgotten my birthday? That was not possible. What hadn't happened once in all these years could not happen now.

But why hadn't they come yet? It was now two minutes past twelve. I was caught up in my thoughts when I heard the familiar whispering and laughter outside the door. I quickly closed my eyes.

'Papa!' The door opened and the cake, flowers and greeting cards joyfully filled my room and my mind. The same mind that a few minutes ago had been thinking all sorts of things in the dark.

As if reading my mind, my elder son Akshay came and sat next to me, 'What's happened, Papa?'

I couldn't lie to him. Slightly sheepishly I said, 'I thought you people had forgotten, that's all,' and looked away guiltily.

Akshay held my hands tightly in his and said, 'How could you think that, Papa? We're your sons, we're just like you, we care about you.'

I breathed deeply and kissed his forehead.

In a little while the boys went to their rooms and I thought about how sensible they both were, and how much they cared about me.

'We're just like you,' Akshay had said. The words touched something deep inside. I was troubled. Were my sons really like me? Had I been a son like them to Babuji?

Sleep had vanished from my eyes. I put my dressing gown on and sat in my rocking chair near the fireplace. My feet sank into the soft fibres of the thick carpet.

This house in a posh locality in London was the result of my life's hard work. When I had come here from India for the first time, I barely had anything—just a few pounds, some nascent dreams and a whole lot of fear. How would I show my face in India if I wasn't successful here?

These days I thought about the old days all the time.

I understand that old age brings with it diseases. But I had called this disease upon myself. This wanting to revisit the old days all the time was disturbing me and making me ill.

I had lived in Jabalpur before I moved to London. Babuji had been a professor in the government college there. We weren't very rich but we lived comfortably. There were the three of us at home, Babuji, Bua and I. Bua had told me that there had been some complications at the time of my birth and my mother had passed away then. I had been with her for three days and then Bua had taken on the role of my mother.

I learnt from other relatives that Babuji and Bua had raised me jointly. And after I grew up a bit, I realized how much I meant to them.

When I was a little older Bua told me that my mother had made Babuji promise that he would never refuse anything I asked for. Maybe that was why Babuji had never married again. I didn't know why Bua had never married, and I hadn't tried to find out.

Today my sons are grown up and when I started thinking about them settling down, I remembered Babuji and his house and Bua. I remembered my mistakes. No matter how hard I tried to shake those memories, I just couldn't.

Maybe I wanted to go back, but who was there to forgive me now?

I woke up the next day with a heavy head. When I asked for an Aspirin with my coffee my sons got worried.

'What's happened, Papa? Is your blood pressure high?' they spoke in unison. One of them placed his palm on my head and asked me, 'Are you feverish? Should we take you to the doctor?'

Their concern annoyed me for some reason and I spoke sharply, 'Nothing has happened bhai! It's just a headache. Please leave me alone!'

Silence filled the room. It was not the custom in my home to leave a sufferer alone. I knew my demand would not be fulfilled so I took the car and drove off.

A little while later I sat on the banks of the Thames. I remembered Gwarighat on the banks of the Narmada River in Jabalpur. I fixed my eyes on the water.

The water was exactly the same. All water is the same, I suppose, but all people aren't the same. I wished Akshay's words were true. I wished I had been a son to Babuji like my sons were to me. I wished I hadn't left Babuji to come and settle in London. I wished I had managed to convince him to come and stay with me here.

Like the way I had convinced him when I had wanted to do the business course in Oxford. And the way I had convinced him to sell his house.

The Thames' banks were crowded.

I remembered the days I had spent with Babuji along the Narmada's banks—when I would go into the water to pick up coins tossed in by the faithful, and Babuji would make me throw them back into deep water telling me that the prayers of found coins aren't answered.

I had never seen Babuji throw a coin into the river. I had, once, with the prayer that Babuji would send me to England to study.

When I sat on Babuji's shoulders so that I could throw the coin into deep waters, I heard Bua, standing on the shore, shout, 'Go further, a little more, a little deeper.'

Three years ago she had shouted in the same way, when I had gone to immerse Babuji's ashes in the river: 'A little further, Bituwa, a little more, a little deeper!'

Evening was falling. This was the first birthday I had spent away from my family. How strange that I suddenly remembered Babuji and Bua and my country.

There was a reason behind this. The reason was the care my sons showed for me, their love for me. These two boys who had grown up abroad were with me at every step. And it was all this that made me feel like a sinner. Maybe I was afraid that I would lose their respect if they found out the truth about me. Would the darkness of the past get hidden with the bright colours of the present?

In my restlessness I called Bua from there itself.

Her frail voice made my throat dry. 'Bua?' Somehow I got the word out.

Her voice grew stronger immediately on hearing mine. 'Bituwa? It's your birthday today. Do you remember?'

She remembered my birthday. I burst into tears, and disconnected the phone.

Every birthday Bua would wake me up early, bathe me and take me to the temple. She would ask Panditji to do a special puja for me, so that nothing bad would ever happen to me again.

And what had I done? I had turned her out of her own home. Babuji had had to sell his house so that I could study abroad. He had spent the last years of his life in a rented house. Where Bua still lived.

Yes, I did send her money every month to fulfil my duty. But today I understood that money transferred into a bank account can never make up for the absence of a child.

The sun was setting across the Thames. India was four and a half hours ahead of London; the sun must have set a long time ago there. It probably set when I had left Babuji and Bua and moved to London.

Staring at the sky I recollected the past. When Babuji would take me boating at a huge waterfall, only so we could see the sunset. He would say, 'This is the only time you see so many shades of orange in the sky; orange, the colour of hope, hope that the sun will rise again tomorrow.' He would tell me stories of that river surrounded by marble rocks. They were all sad stories.

I felt restless. Heavy-headed. I called my travel agent. 'A ticket for next week. No, not a return; a one-way.'

I felt some peace after I put the phone down. I went home. They must be waiting for me for my birthday party.

That night when I told my wife and children about my plan to go to India, they were shocked. My wife said, 'What is the need now? Babuji isn't here any more and you send money to Buaji every month.'

My sons were quiet. Then after a while Akshay spoke, 'If you want to go you should.' And the younger one joined him, 'You must go, Papa.'

Something inside me hurt. Whenever my children said 'Yes, Papa,' agreeing to something I said, I heard my own spoilt insistence, 'No, Babuji, no.'

Every good thing about my sons showed me all my mistakes, made me remember Babuji and Bua.

When I had first mentioned wanting to go abroad, after two years with an IT firm in India, it had made Babuji deeply uneasy. I didn't realize it then but it was the fear of losing his son.

I had convinced myself that it was the pain of having to sell his house to arrange the money for me. Maybe that's why I assuaged my mind by sending him money.

But the wounds I inflicted had deepened and I had remained oblivious.

When I landed in Jabalpur it was eight in the morning. I caught a taxi and went home. The last time I had been here was when Babuji had died. And I had come for a week two or three years before that.

As I entered the house I was welcomed with the fragrance of incense. I had forgotten how the perfumed air could touch your mind. I pushed open the door to see Bua praying to the tulsi plant.

Seeing me she left her puja midway and ran to me and clung to me. She softly said, 'You'll stay a few days? You don't have to leave early?'

I enveloped Bua, in her crushed and worn sari and her fragrance of sandalwood, tightly in my arms. 'I won't go, Bua, not soon.'

After crying for a while Bua asked if I wanted water. Then she made me a cup of strong tea. She had my luggage placed in Babuji's room. The cupboard in his room was still filled with his things: his glasses, calculator, diary and pen. I put my glasses and my phone and my pen next to his things. His photograph hung on the wall, the one with him and my mother, their wedding photograph.

I ate my food and left the house. I had something urgent to do.

I walked down the alley to its other end, to the house in which I had spent my childhood. Whose mango tree bore the raw mangoes from which *panna* was made to save me from the Loo that blew in the hot summer months. The house that I had caused to be sold.

I stopped in front of the house. It was in a bad condition, the plaster peeling, the mango tree covered in dust. I wondered if it still bore fruit.

There was a brick boundary wall outside the house. It hadn't been there before. Earlier, a thick grove of henna had been enough; green and fragrant, it had looked so lovely. When homes become houses, their greenery goes away, and their perfume.

I went home. Bua had made *gatte ki sabzi* and roti and was waiting for me. She remembered what I liked to eat, she remembered everything.

For the first few days she cooked for me and we talked about Babuji and my childhood. The thing that pained me the most was that she had no complaint against me. Nothing she said showed me that Babuji had been upset with me, or disappointed in me,

In a few days I had accomplished the task that I had come for. I was the owner of Babuji's house, my house. The papers of the house felt like Babuji's caress and my mind's burden lessened a little.

I took the papers to Bua and smiled as I put them in her lap. She looked at the papers but didn't say anything for a long time, then softly she said, 'Why did you spend so much money? I am okay here.'

I was surprised. I had thought Bua would dance for joy when she got the papers and run and place them in her mandir. I thought she would hug me and heap the blessings of the world on me. And then she would rush to make something sweet and stuff it down my throat.

But it hadn't happened like that. She just got up and went quietly to her room. When the house had been sold too she and Babuji had been calm like this.

I remained sitting in the courtyard. I realized that I hadn't ever really understood Babuji and Bua. It was I who had been important for them. The house was irrelevant then and it was irrelevant now.

But now I knew what I had to do.

Some weeks later Bua and I were clearing the security check for our flight to London at Delhi's International Airport. I smiled as I watched Bua arrange her *badi* and pickle packets.

The sparkle in her eyes and the joy that filled her face were like a soft balm on old wounds.

NAILS

Umesh Pant

The engagement had just finished, signs of it lay littered around the room. On the tables teacups and empty plates waited to be cleared away. My cousins were examining the gifts I had been given and my friends were teasing me about Sumit, who had become my fiancé from being my boyfriend and who had just left for office. Ma was complaining, 'He could have taken a whole day off for his own engagement at least.' I had tried to explain to her that he had an important meeting that he couldn't get out of, but would she understand? And how could I expect her to understand? Nothing was usual about our relationship. Even today Sumit and I are more friends than lovers, we live in the same house, dream the same dreams, live the same lives, a life in which we are equal.

Many things had changed since we had first declared our love, and we viewed those changes as achievements.

When we first met we both had twenty-five-thousand-rupee jobs. We lived next door to each other in rented rooms in Munirka and shared a bathroom. We both went to our respective offices in DTC buses and stopped together on the way home to enjoy a qawwali at Nizammudin or to spin dreams at the Qutb Minar in Mehrauli. Sometimes I would forget my religious beliefs and eat some gravy from his plate of chicken curry and sometimes he would toss aside the nonvegetarian menu in a restaurant and ask, 'What is your vegetarian speciality?' In those days late-night auto rickshaw rides were a luxury.

We were both software engineers which is how we got to know each other. Soon we were neighbours and then we were in love. We now going to put the stamp of society's approval on our four-year-old love story. But as our engagement concluded something had happened that made me question if we were doing the right thing.

Our families had been sitting around when Sumit drew out a beautiful blue engagement ring from his pocket. I extended my left hand. He hesitated and looked at my hand strangely and then at me.

'What?' I asked.

'Nothing,' he said and slipped the ring on to my finger. I put my ring on his finger and whispered in his ear, 'Congratulations, Mister Sumit! You are going to become a husband!'

He smiled in response but it had been a bland smile. His response to my congratulations was, 'Yaar, the least you could have done was cut your nails. You know *I don't like* these long nails.'

'Why are you ruining your mood for such a small thing, and on a day like today?' I tried to make light of the matter. But Sumit seemed to be more upset then he looked.

'It's not just a matter of a nail, Simmi,' he said.

It certainly wasn't, I thought. If my nail could have caused him so much trouble, there must be something triggering the strong reaction.

Was it my nail that had annoyed him, or the fact that I had not listened to him? If it was the first reason it was okay but it was the second?

We had just got engaged, then why had the relationship that had grown over four years suddenly started seeming weak to me, over an insignificant nail?

'Where are you lost, Simmi? Your phone is ringing,' Ma's words broke into my thoughts. It was Sumit. I picked up the phone and heard Sumit's voice on the other end. 'Could I speak to my soon-to-be-wife, please?'

'She's busy at the moment. Please leave a message and it will be delivered,' I replied.

'Please tell her that I will be late today and that she should have her dinner and sleep.' And he hung up. There was a hackathon in his office that day and no one would leave till all the work was finished. He was presenting a new software idea and if it was selected he would win a trip to Paris. I had been very excited for Sumit, but suddenly I found myself wishing he didn't win the contest.

It wasn't that I didn't want him to win. I knew I wouldn't be able to get long leave within the next two months. The thought hadn't crossed my mind earlier. But suddenly I was wondering what would happen if he won the contest and I couldn't go to Paris with him. I had always believed that Sumit would respect his happiness but at the same time he would also understand my constraints.

I couldn't get Sumit's expression as he had looked at my nails out of my head.

I took the car out and drove mindlessly around. Whenever I needed time to think alone I would drive out to unknown roads. I sit in a new cafe. It's as if the strangeness of the new place brings me closer to the familiar. I find it easy to talk to myself.

I was sitting alone in a cafe again.

The shine seemed to have gone out of the dreams I had seen of a future with Sumit. The weather reflected my confusion, it couldn't decide whether it was going to be sunny, or rain.

Ma had taken a long time to try and explain things to me.

'Look, Simmi, you have decided who you want to marry and we haven't objected; we compromised on our views on caste and arranged marriage. Marriage is all about compromise; you will have to learn to adjust.'

How could I explain to Ma that the thing that had drawn me to Sumit was the fact that I didn't have to adjust myself for him. I had stayed how I was and that was how Sumit had fallen in love with me. And he had stayed how he was. We had never tried to change each other. So how is it a small thing if this crucial thing has changed now?

Since my childhood I had rebelled for all sorts of things, including my nail.

The first time I had bought a new nail polish and worn it to school, the teacher had noticed it immediately. 'Simmi, nice girls don't grow their nails so long. Cut them and come to school tomorrow.'

Then I made the mistake of asking her, 'What is the correlation between long nails and goodness, ma'am?'

She looked at me in disbelief, amazed that I had asked the question. I knew that one shouldn't have long nails for hygiene purposes. But I had only grown the nail of one finger. And I always kept it clean. I really wanted to know how one became good if one kept their nails short.

My teacher had slapped me for asking the question. Even then the question had not been of the nail. It had been my questioning her authority.

Why had such a small incident created this storm in my mind? Was I making too much out of it?

For a while now I had not been able to imagine a life without Sumit. He used to drop me to office every morning and pick me up every evening. When he didn't have the car I used to pick him up in an autorickshaw on the way home. We had both wanted a car but neither of us could afford one. When I had got my first proper bonus after my promotion it had been my suggestion that we both jointly buy a car, 'I'll make the down payment, you pay the EMIs,' I had suggested.

It seemed to trouble him a bit and then he brushed it off lightly saying, 'No, yaar! I'm not going to buy my first car with my girlfriend's money! I'm not that badly off!'

But I had insisted.

'Come on, Sumit. We are going to marry each other. How does it matter?'

I had managed to convince him somehow. After that we both joined the same driving school and learnt how to drive. But I couldn't remember a single occasion when I had sat in the driver's seat. For the first time in years I wondered, why was Sumit always in the driver's seat?

As I sat alone in the cafe, I looked back at all those moments through new eyes. I had been flowing freely, pushed along by some current. It was the flow of love, where nothing is questioned. I was a wave. But all waves don't make it to the shore. And I was stuck in the middle of the sea now.

'Simmi, what are you doing here?'

The familiar voice made me turn around. It was a friend from college, Parul. Parul came with all sorts of memories.

'Remember how we made a sudden programme and went up to Nainital?'

'And remember that golgappa guy who gave us two extra golgappas every day?'

Parul was a trunk full of memories. Her words were like a mirror that showed me my old self. The Simmi who could disappear from the city for a week without a care, the girl who loved the fragrance of the mountains.

'Remember how you used to want to go to the mountains just before the first rains of the season? We saw so many mountain rains like that, yaar. What days those were!'

Where was the Simmi that was crazy about paragliding and bungee jumping? Where had she gone? I couldn't understand.

After speaking with Parul I tried to look for the girl that I had been before I met Sumit. I looked but I couldn't find her.

'How was the engagement? You'll be Mrs So-and-So in a few days! Will you change your surname?'

Parul was a lot more excited about my engagement than I was.

'You're lucky, yaar. You're getting to marry the guy you love.'

Was I really marrying the guy I loved? I hoped Parul was right. I hoped this was the same Sumit who I had fallen in love with.

I reached home in a scattered state that day to find my house as scattered as I was. I couldn't decided whether I should first sort out the house or myself. All the relatives that had come for the engagement had left adequate proof of their having being there. The place was strewn with towels and polythene. My cousin had left the contents of my make-up box strewn across the dressing table. Next to the lipstick and the eyeliner was the bottle of nail polish that still sparkled on my nail. As I picked everything up to put away in the cupboard, I noticed a nail cutter.

What will happen if I just cut this stupid nail? Is it really such a big thing? I picked up the nail cutter and went and sat on the sofa.

'I hope you remain the same after you get married!'

Parul's words as she had left echoed in my mind. I felt as if something was plugged in my brain.

There was a knock at the door. Sumit opened the door and came in. He gave me a washed-out smile.

'Please give me some water quickly, if possible some orange juice.'

He didn't look at me as he said it, as if I was sitting around waiting for his order. Then his gaze fell on the nail cutter in my right hand.

'Oh, good! You cut your nail.'

He spoke casually. As if he knew that that was what would happen. But something in the tone of his voice hit my heart like a missile. There is a fine line between compromising and adjusting. If you change because you want to it doesn't hurt, but if you need to change to suit someone else's wishes than that can be come unbearable.

I put the nail cutter on the table and went up to Sumit. I looked him in the eye and said, 'Let's put the wedding on hold for a while, Sumit. I need some time to think.'

'What?' He was shocked.

'Are you mad? The date will be fixed in a few days and you want time?' Wordlessly I began to take the ring off my finger. His gaze fell on my nail and I think he understood. He had always claimed to understand me better than even I could.

'You want to put the wedding on hold for such a small thing? I mean, for one nail?' He was astounded.

'It isn't about the nail, Sumit,' I said looking into his eyes and left the ring on the table.

The ring lay on the table next to the nail cutter. I looked at Sumit and then left the room. Sumit was still looking at the ring and the nail cutter.

THE SEAL

Anulata Raj Nair

The brightness of Eid decorations lit up the Chowk Bazaar. Colourful dupattas decorated the shops, some studded with sequins, others lined with thin borders of golden gota. People thronged the shops that sold crochet caps, bent over the wares. The tailors were the busiest, their machines stitching masses of kurtas and pyjamas and sherwanis. The clatter of the sewing machines melded with the sound of the azan. The lanes were full of the colour and tinkle of glass bangles. The chowk felt different during Ramadan, divine, as if the air was filled the perfume of prayers.

I stopped my official jeep at the head of the lane and walked down. Every step that took me forward in those narrow lanes took my mind ten years back.

I had spent my childhood in this area in old Bhopal, in Ibrahimpura. Whatever I achieved in life I found here, and the blame for all I lost is on these lanes too.

'Sahab, will you have some sherbet or something else cold?' my orderly, walking behind me, asked.

'No, no, I'll get something for myself, you stay in the car,' I told him, and walking fast, entered a very narrow lane, which held my childhood, where I grew up.

I stopped in front of a shop. It didn't have a name, just a board that said 'urgent stamps'. Outside, some nameplates swung with the wind: brass, wooden and ordinary painted ones.

Strewn on the table were all sorts of seals: small ones, big ones, round ones and square ones. I turned one over. I'm not sure what was written on it but to me it looked like my name: 'Aman Kumar Agarwal, Judicial Officer, First Class'.

The shopkeeper looked at me intently. Maybe I was a customer. But I disappointed him and walked to the far end of the lane and stopped in front of my old house.

It almost looked as if the house too felt the sorrow of our having left it. The paint on the doors was faded, the hinges were rusted and the cracks had widened. Inside, there was nothing for me to peep in to see.

The next house was closed. Pipal saplings were growing from the cracks in its rotting wood beams, their leaves proclaiming that no one lived there any more. Ignoring the lock on the door, I knocked a special knock.

But there was no sound of feet running to the door in recognition of that knock. I felt like calling out her name, but the word seemed to get stuck in my throat.

I don't know how long I stood there. 'Why am I here?' I asked myself. 'Who am I looking for?'

It had been six years since I had been here, in this lane where my house stood—where Babuji had his shop, a seal shop.

I was trying to relive those long-gone days that crammed this narrow lane filled with memories.

Babuji had raised me alone. I had never missed having a mother, and if ever I did, Paro's mother had filled that emptiness for me. I just needed to climb over the courtyard wall to reach her.

Paro and I were the same age. We had started school together. We had the same bag, the same uniform, the same tiffin box, everything was the same. Except us. I hated studying. I only studied for a few hours after Babuji came home, out of fear. Paro could spend the whole day buried in her books.

It was a different story when the results came. I somehow always did better than her. She would get angry looking at my mark sheet. Tugging at her mother's sari she would wail, 'How has he got better marks, Ma? Tell me! He doesn't even study!'

Once, to make her happy, I had struck out my name on my mark sheet and written hers instead.

The same story continued till we were in the tenth grade. I only studied out of fear of Babuji and she spent her whole day studying.

But something had started to change. Our relationship.

Somewhere between sixteen and seventeen my heart began to race at the mention of Paro. And I'm certain it was the same for her. Now when I got more marks than her,

her eyes would light up and she would pat my back and say, 'You really are intelligent, one day you will become a big officer.'

But I ignored her praise and her shining eyes. I looked for the smile on her lips. I wanted to feel the softness of her hands.

I was taking becoming useless in love to new heights. I had never really been interested in studies and now I only wanted to study enough to pass. I didn't feel the need to study.

I managed to scrape through twelfth grade somehow and went straight to Babuji's shop from school. Paro was with me. I had purposely taken her along.

At the shop, with pride I announced grandly that from now on I was going to sit in the shop, work, earn money.

After having my say I looked at both of them, expecting praise and encouragement.

But I was shocked when Babuji shouted, 'Are you mad! I'm not educating you so that you can spend your life in this small shop! Do you understand?'

And Paro, she snatched her hand out of mine and ran out of the shop.

Paro was the first page of my love story.

In those days when the rest of the boys were up on the roof flying kites I was sitting on the courtyard wall gazing at Paro, and when after a long time she finally noticed me and looked at me, I felt like I had won a lottery. At that time there was no bigger bumper prize for me than winning over Paro.

But that day when she had run away from Babuji's shop, she had left me penniless. It was for her that I had decided to look after the shop. I wanted to show her that I was sensible and responsible. I couldn't understand what I had done wrong.

After Paro left, Babuji had held my shoulders and sat me down on the thin bench in the shop. I could feel his hands trembling.

In a voice full of emotion he had said, 'I have big dreams for you, son. Every time I made a seal for any officer I always saw your name in those letters. Engineer Aman Kumar Agarwal, or Doctor Aman, or IAS Aman.'

I stared at Babuji. What language was he speaking? I was shocked that a man who sat in such a small shop, a maker of seals, when did he start to see such big dreams? Why?

Babuji held my hand in his firm hands, 'Paro says that you get such good marks when you study even for an hour; if you study hard you will definitely become a senior officer.'

I was angry. Paro and I were happy together. Why was my kite now suddenly flying towards a good career? How had the wind changed?

Irritated I got up and left the shop midway between Babuji's sentence. I went straight to Paro's house. She was in the courtyard reading a book on a rug. I went and sat in front of her and said angrily, 'What is this officer business? I'm not going to study for twenty-four hours a day, understand that.' And I got up to walk away.

She called out from behind me, 'You understand this too then. I'm not going to spend my life with some guy who makes seals and stamps. I'm going to marry a guy who has his own seal.'

After that day, our relationship changed. I stopped staring at her from the roof. She also came over less with laddoos and *sewai* made by her mother. We hadn't stopped talking, but it wasn't comfortable like before.

Without really wanting to I too started spending more and more time with my books. My evenings were now spent in the Central Library on Itwara Road. Babuji couldn't afford to buy all the books I needed. And sitting in the library saved me from thoughts of Paro. The thick walls of the 110-year-old building built by the nawabs seemed to be able to keep thoughts out as well. The scent of the old books snuffed out the perfume of Paro's wrists.

I began to prepare for the civil service examinations along with my bachelor's degree. I don't know how Paro felt but I still loved her. My love had just moved from centre stage to the background.

One winter evening it was particularly dark. As I entered the lane on my way back from the library Paro appeared suddenly and grabbed my wrist. I stopped.

There was something in her eyes that I couldn't understand. Then she laughed softly and said, 'I wish one could get married just by holding hands.'

I didn't understand so I stayed quiet.

I think she didn't like my silence. 'Say something at least!'

I smiled and said, 'We can hold hands and take the seven *phera*s. We'll be married.'

She laughed and said, 'We need a stamp, sir, for a wedding, an official seal.'

And in a second she had run away to other end of the lane.

I tried to understand if there was something unsaid in her laughter.

I was engaged in preparation for the civil services but I didn't want to study, that was certain. I was doing it for Paro because we needed a seal to be married. I was doing it for Babuji. Because he wanted me to be a big officer, an officer with his own seal, his own stamp.

What a strange longing his was. When after the whole day I would return home he would tell me as he served me my food, 'Today I made a nameplate for an SP. He's a retired officer. And I made a seal for him. With his son's name.'

I could see the dampness in his eyes as he would tell me these stories. I knew him very well. I just couldn't understand why he got so hopeless when he saw me in the shop he loved.

And Paro, she was even stranger. She had big dreams; she wanted to do a course in fashion design and was studying hard for it. She knew what she wanted.

Sometimes we would sit on the wall of the roof and talk. Neither of us had ever seriously expressed our love for each other. But I knew there was love. Some truths are like that, they claim their existence without any evidence.

It was at her insistence that I had started studying.

She had started to bring me things to eat again: besan laddoos, soaked almonds, thick creamy kheer. I wish I could have found a way of knowing if she brought them herself or if her mother sent them. But I never found out. Because I never asked.

Sometimes we would sit on the roof till nightfall. On seeing the first star she would always mumble something. I would smile at her childishness. Sometimes in the dark our shoulders would touch. I still don't know why I never held her in my arms. Maybe I knew it was necessary for her that I became an officer and that stopped me.

Finally the results were out. I was not selected.

That year was the worst year of my life. I broke inside.

It was then that Paro got admission in a college in Mumbai and she left. She was so happy that the happiness numbed the pain of our separation.

She didn't say much when she came to say goodbye, no promises, no expressed hope to meet again.

It was as if I had imagined her love. Maybe I had.

I had lost all confidence in myself so it was inappropriate for me to say anything. After Paro left I really became like Devdas. I didn't want to go to the library. It hurt to step out of the house.

I began to sit in the shop again. I made number plates for cars. I ran my fingers over the important designations on nameplates and set them aside, I saw the names etched on seals . . .

I knew Babuji hated my sitting in the shop but I ignored it.

I may have spent my life there in the shop but one day Babuji came into my room. He had a beautiful seal with my name on it in his hands.

I looked at my name stamped in red on the white paper in front of me. I looked at him. I think he had a lot to say, but all he said was, 'Try once more, son, I've made this for you . . .'

'Sir, should I get you some tea?' my orderly's voice surprised me. I looked at my watch. I had gone back so many years in an hour.

I started for home. Babuji was waiting for me at my official residence.

Since my posting in this city I come here whenever I can. Maybe in the hope that on the bend in that narrow lane Paro will grab my wrist and pull me towards her and we will be standing face to face again.

As I reached home and looked at the veranda I couldn't believe my eyes.

She was standing there, smiling, that same smile that lit up her eyes.

I wanted to ask her so much, but all I could manage was 'Where are you these days? How come you're here?'

Without saying a word she took some papers out of her bag and said, 'I need your stamp on my marriage certificate.'

I felt a bitterness in my throat.

Babuji put his hand on her head and said, 'He's become somebody because of you.'

She laughed and said, 'Yes, Babuji, I always told him a seal was needed for marriage!'

I stamped her papers in silence.

She sat across from me. I looked for a trace of tears in her eyes.

A DIVORCED GIRL

Jamshed Qamar Siddiqui

Is it just me or is it a universal truth that the hands of a clock move considerably faster in the morning? That morning had been the same crazy running-around kind of morning. I kept glancing at the clock as I prepared lunchboxes for my five-year-old son Akshay and myself.

'Mummy, my English writing book,' Akshay called out and I stuck my head out of the kitchen and said, 'You did your homework on the sofa yesterday; it must be there. How many times have I told you to pack your bag the previous night?' I had barely finished speaking when my cell phone rang and I now spoke with it scrunched between my ear and my shoulder.

'Hello, Mummy! Yes! Yes! Listen, I'm getting late for office, I'll call you from there. Yes, your grandson has had his breakfast! Yes, I've given him his almonds! I'm putting the phone down now otherwise I'll be late again. Okay, bye!'

I gave Akshay his breakfast and stood in front of the mirror to do my hair. I undid the bun and started brushing fast. While disentangling some knotted strands I noticed the dark circles that had appeared under my eyes. I touched them. It looked as if all the nights I had spent alone had collected beneath my eyes. I looked at my burdened eyes and tired face, but whatever else there was or wasn't certainly was self-belief.

I rode the scooty at a slow pace, but Akshay clung to me tightly. A pink helmet on my head, I wended my way slowly through the traffic like a novice. I was a novice. I wasn't used to it yet. It had been only two months since I had sold the car. There was no real need for a car now. Also, one had to be more cautious when one travelled alone along life's highways.

I had got divorced four years ago. Since then Akshay had been my sole responsibility. Everything was my sole responsibility. From the society meetings to bank work to making the rations list and Akshay's parent–teacher meetings, I had surrounded myself with so much work that the weight of memories was beginning to lessen. It's true, though, it was still as hard as it had always been to answer Akshay's innocent questions. It had been hard even when we couldn't scale the walls of silence. I could read the sadness that descended in his eyes when he watched the other children playing with their fathers in the evenings.

'Where were you? Ashwini sir has asked twice already for you!' my colleague Neha said in a flutter. I put my bag down on my desk and drew a deep breath. Then I drank two glasses of water from the dispenser close by. This was the second time I was late this week. Anyway, what could be done about it? *Help me, God*, I thought and set off towards the boss's cabin. In any case, no excuse would stand a chance in the face of Ashwini sir's temper.

'May I come in, sir?' I asked with as much gentleness and sweetness as I could muster, as if he might melt on hearing my voice.

Ashwini sir looked over his frameless glasses and said, 'Yes, come in. Sit.' A little fearfully I sat on one of the two chairs in front of him. I don't know if the AC in his cabin was unusually effective or whether I was scared, but I felt slightly cold.

'Are the papers for the deal ready?' he pushed a file aside as he asked. 'There is a client visit this evening; I hope we are ready?' I answered, flustered, 'Yes, sir, the papers are ready, I'll just show them to you.'

'Okay, great!' he said, before looking at the clock. 'So you're late again, huh?' My heart stopped beating. 'Actually, sir, you know . . . ' He cut me short. 'No, no, it's okay, Gaurav told me you were working late in office last night. It's fine. But don't forget to take care of yourself either. Don't fall sick. This month is crucial for us.'

Late last night? But I had left in the evening. I controlled my expressions, thanked him and left the cabin. I inhaled deeply. 'Won't you say thanks?' a familiar voice surprised me. Gaurav sir was standing right in front of me.

Gaurav sir was my senior at work. I reported to him and he in turn reported to Ashwini sir. Gaurav sir was serious, focused and very professional as far as work was concerned.

He was a very helpful colleague. He often tried to be more of a friend than a boss. He knew I was divorced. At first I thought he offered help out of sympathy, but slowly I got the feeling that his feelings for me were beyond that.

I tried to maintain distance every time he tried to come close. But I had to thank him for what he had done.

'Thanks, sir,' I said and he replied, 'It's okay, I know you got late dropping Akshay to school.'

I nodded and he asked, 'How is Akshay?'

I think he wanted to talk more but I said, 'He's fine,' and pulled my chair out, sat down and started working. I watched his reflection on my computer screen. He stood behind me for a while and then left.

The world looks differently at a divorced girl. Every gaze is either trying to figure out her previous relationship or see the possibility of her next. Forget the world; my own mother had the same worry. Every phone call would be about four new eligible matches: 'Beta, you can't live life alone.'

Gaurav sir was really nice, decent, but I just didn't have the courage. I think I had forgotten how to trust, how to blindly hand myself over completely to someone. On life's mirror, even the smallest cracks appeared as a lesson. Maybe that was why living alone seemed a better prospect to me than holding my hand out to someone or taking a hand that was being held out to me.

Often we are not alone even when we think we are and sometimes we are alone even when we are with someone. Being alone while being with someone is the most hollow feeling in the world, and I had experienced it. And perhaps it was because of that feeling that I didn't want to take any step in my life that could make me even more alone.

One night it was raining hard. It was at about 1.30 a.m. that Akshay had started vomiting. I touched his forehead; he was burning with fever. I called several doctors but none were willing to come out in the rain. Akshay's condition was worsening. I finally called Neha. 'Listen, don't worry, I'll be there soon,' she said and hung up. The rain was falling harder now. Every crash of thunder shook me deep inside. Every flash of lightning reflected off the balcony wall and I held Akshay's hand tighter.

I understood the pain of loneliness very acutely that night. Akshay lay in my lap as tears filled my eyes. It was an unbearable helplessness—I couldn't do anything, and nothing was in my hands. Seconds later the bell rang. The sound filled me with hope: Neha had come. I ran as fast as I could and opened the door.

It was Gaurav sir.

'How is he? Let's get him to the hospital quickly,' he said as he stepped past me and entered my house. I stood at the door, confused.

As he drove the car through heavy rain he told me that Neha had called him. He tried to comfort me, 'Don't worry, we're almost there.' Akshay's head was on my lap, and I could see nothing, think of nothing beyond him.

We reached the hospital and headed straight to the children's ward. After a few injections and a drip, Akshay's condition started to improve. Soon he fell asleep, and on the wooden stool near his bed sat Gaurav sir. He spent the whole night sitting there.

The next day Gaurav sir dropped us home and as he left he said, 'I'm leaving now. Don't worry about work; I'll handle it. Let me know if you need anything.'

I had no way to thank him for what he had done, and I didn't think life would give me a chance to thank him either. I stopped near his car window and, looking into his eyes, I asked him, 'Why are you doing all this?' He looked surprised, and then after a moment's thought he said, 'I don't know. But it could be that what you are thinking is in fact the reason. Who knows what fate has in store? See you!'

He left in a cloud of dust, and I looked through my tears at the crooked lines on my palms that seemed to tell me nothing.

My mother arrived by the evening train. She was relieved to find Akshay well but I kept seeing Gaurav sir in her questions. 'Thank God he came. What would have happened if he hadn't? Where do you find people like that these days?' I understood what she was trying to say, what her words implied. It wasn't restricted only to Ma. At office, too, Neha kept saying the same thing; everything always became about Gaurav sir.

I don't what it was, but everyone was in a hurry to reach the conclusion from which I was trying hard to run away. I knew what those two well-wishers were trying to say, but I just didn't want to understand. I didn't want to be with anyone. For some reason the world seemed to see me as incomplete, not whole. Maybe it was not only me, maybe every divorced girl is looked upon like that. Every girl who is alone is viewed as incomplete.

That day Gaurav sir didn't come to office. Every time I looked at his empty chair, questions filled my mind. In the midst of all this I was thrilled to hear that my promotion had been confirmed. After a long time I really smiled; it felt like a ray of light was shining through the dark clouds.

Everyone at work was congratulating me, someone asked for a party, someone for a treat. Only Neha stood out, her face bore no happiness. She wished me half-heartedly and then returned to her work.

'What's happened, Neha? You look troubled,' I said.

Tidying her hair, she replied, 'No, nothing like that.'

I sat down on the chair near hers and asked, 'Doesn't look like it, and congratulations to you too! Ashwini sir is sending you to the Pune conference!'

As I spoke her hands stopped moving across the keyboard, 'No, yaar, I'm not going, Vinay is going now.'

'But why?' I asked.

'Gaurav sir said it would be better if a male employee went,' she replied.

I felt really bad when I heard that. Gaurav sir had got Neha's visit cancelled. He thought it would be safer to send a male employee to a new city. This wasn't the first time this had happened. He usually preferred to assign outdoor work to male employees. I felt terrible for Neha.

Anyway, I reached home that evening and rang the bell. I had bought cake for Ma and Akshay. I was impatient to tell them about the promotion, and rang the doorbell quite a few times in my excitement. I had thought that as soon as Ma opened the door I would hold the cake out and yell, 'Surprise!'

The door opened and all I managed to get out was the 'S . . .' My smile froze. Gaurav sir was at the door.

'Sir! You, here?' I stammered. He smiled and replied, 'Yes, I came to visit Akshay. I was coming to office but Aunty stopped me!' Smiling he stood aside to let me enter. Ma and Akshay were both in the drawing room. I glared at Ma and went into another room.

Why was all this happening to me? Why is life so difficult? The problem was that I couldn't hate Gaurav sir. It would have been easy if I could. I knew what he felt for me was well intentioned. Maybe that's why I was finding it hard to push him away.

When I entered the drawing room after a while I found Akshay playing with Gaurav sir. I think he was trying to teach him how to tell the time. 'So, if the small one is at three and the big one at two, it's ten minutes past three.'

Their laughter seemed to fill that sad room with perfume. The old silences were slowly being replaced. Hopelessness was fading. And sitting in a corner Ma was smiling.

After Gaurav sir left, I worked in the kitchen for quite some time. Ma came up to me and said, 'He's a nice boy. What is your problem? If not for yourself, at least think about Akshay.' I was shocked to hear these words. I didn't realize she was thinking so far ahead. But then I understood why. In my absence he must have asked Ma for my hand in marriage. She had not said anything but she wanted me to say yes.

I knew that everything that was happening around me was for the good. Ma was not wrong. But something stopped me from crossing the threshold into a new relationship. Maybe it was a fear that only someone who had lost something precious would understand. But now the silence around me was questioning me. There were doubts. There were possibilities. And something was pulling me away from my own convictions. But most of all it was the happiness I saw in Akshay's face after so long.

I believe that it is not we ourselves but our circumstances that take decisions for us. And once again that happened. I didn't sleep that night. I stood at the window watching the night's darkness meet the morning's light. I accepted the proposal.

In that one day my life changed. I had never seen Ma so excited and full of life. The few people who knew about it in office couldn't stop congratulating me. Some relatives called to say, 'After all, how long could you have lived alone? Good, now you'll have some support.'

Support. That was the reason I had avoided taking this decision for so long. I knew the society I lived in thought this way about divorced girls. No one thought they needed love, but only support.

I don't know whether it was love or support, but life suddenly opened up like a window. I noticed a pleasant change in myself too. It wasn't so bad, this decision. The roadside flower shop, happy children coming home from school, the birds flying in the sky, everything suddenly looked good.

One evening, Gaurav sir—whom I now called Gaurav at his insistence—and I were sitting in the coffee house near the office. We smiled at each other from across the table. After the first sip of coffee Gaurav pushed a bunch of keys towards me. 'What is this?' I asked, surprised. 'My car keys. They're yours from today.' 'Why?' I asked. 'I live so close to office, I can just take an auto,' he said.

'That's okay, Gaurav. But, no, please, you keep them; I prefer the scooty.' I said no again and he replied very seriously, 'Actually, I don't like that you ride that scooty; all sorts of people look at you in all sorts of ways. Well, it might have been okay before, but now I certainly don't feel comfortable. Please take the keys.'

I watched him in silence. I hadn't expected that reply. I was shocked. Gaurav covered my hand with his and said, 'And anyway, this isn't forever. After we are married I won't let you sweat away in that good-for-nothing office. You enjoy your life, look after Akshay, all the other responsibilities will be mine.'

I felt tears welling up in my eyes. In one second it felt as if all of society had compressed itself into that chair in front of me, in Gaurav's image. When with trembling lips I told him that I wanted to continue to work after marriage he began to explain to me all the ills in the world and the character of the people in the office. I watched the growing love in his eyes, the love that would ask me to give up everything in return.

Like society, Gaurav too felt that he was doing me a favour by marrying me, and that in my gratitude I would do whatever he asked of me.

I pushed the keys back towards him and stood up. 'I'm going,' I said.

'But what happened? I don't understand!' he stammered.

'It's not necessary that you understand everything. I couldn't understand you, and I am not who you understood me to be.'

Gaurav's forehead was furrowed with confusion. He couldn't believe what had just happened. Divorced women didn't say no.

'I wanted companionship, Gaurav, not support. I can't go ahead with this marriage,' I told him.

He stood up. I turned and left. I didn't look back and he didn't call out to me. Once outside, I began to walk along the side of the road. I was walking so fast my breathing was fast and heavy, my hair flew wildly around my face. People stared at me. I walked on. After many days I felt whole. I had left my incompleteness behind, on that table, with the bunch of keys.

UMRAO JAAN

Manjit Thakur

The nearest town in this coal-mining area is Asansol. The breeze that clings to the coal mines brings heat and fine grains of coal with it. In the summer, the place heats up like a hot pan. Men are so bathed in sweat that it becomes unbearable. It was hot like that today. Priyamvad, oblivious to it all, sat on a cane bench at a tea stall, uneasy, impatient.

The half-moon warned of its imminent departure. For some reason it looked useless and worthless to Priyamvad today.

Usually after two glasses of strong tea Priyamvad would perk up and hum all the way back to his flat, but today was different.

Who could he share his heart's pain with? Ever since that gorgeous face had passed his way, nothing else looked nice. It had only been three days but it felt like it had been an age since he had seen it. Priyamvad realized today what stuff love was made of.

95

The start of his love story had been with the most unlikely person, a person of little worth, someone he would not normally have looked twice at.

It had happened just three days ago.

This worthless fellow named Guddu was a pimp, in the business of providing dancing girls for weddings. The evening had been gathering around and seeing Priyamvad alone in the deepening darkness at the tea stall he had sidled up to him and asked, 'Sahab, want to have some fun?'

Priyamvad was a sophisticated sort of person. He was managing a mining project in a coal mine that bordered Jharkhand and West Bengal. Sometimes, to escape his loneliness and boredom, he would venture into the town's bazaar. If nothing else, he would drink milky tea from the dusty glasses at the tea stall, and then meander back to his bungalow. The bungalow was surrounded by trees that had grown from the coal dust. In that tree-filled oasis, you saw no one, not even a bird.

If he discounted his servants, he felt like Robinson Crusoe marooned on a deserted island. He would come home and eat the tasteless food cooked by his servant and fall asleep. The next day would be the same, arguing with the foreman and labourers about the work never being done on time.

Priyamvad looked disdainfully at him and said, 'Fun? What fun?'

And then, as if extending an invitation, that man drew right up to him and said, 'Would you like to hear a mujra, Sahab? Mujra! Exactly like Umrao Jaan!'

Priyamvad looked at something in the distance. Then after some thought he went with that fellow whose cracked heels forced him to hobble along.

He brought Priyamvad to a narrow lane where on a panelled wooden door with peeling blue paint a name had been scratched: Umrao Jaan.

Something about that name drew him. He had many associations with that name: a delicate girl like the actress Rekha, who would offer him an elegant salaam, and when she sang her voice would be sweet like Asha Bhosle's. The hall where she would sing and dance would be draped with garlands of jasmine. He followed Guddu up the stairs.

The sound of singing emanated from the top floor of the house: a slightly off-key voice singing 'Tip Tip Barsa Pani' to the accompaniment of a harmonium and a tabla. As Priyamvad entered through the doorway the picture he had imagined shattered into a million pieces.

Guddu showed him to a seat. Dust accompanied the creases of moonlight that spread across the floor. Many men sat or lounged around. 'Tip Tip Barsa Pani' had come to an end.

A new girl walked in.

The first thing she did was to inspect her audience. She noticed that the new catch had some contempt in his eyes. She cleared her throat and began to sing, '*Dekha hai pehli baar, saajan ki aankhon mein pyar.*' I see love for the first time in the eyes of my beloved.

Priyamvad was irritated. He looked for Guddu who had disappeared. Probably in search of another customer.

The cheap atmosphere, the girls' disreputable clothes and the people sitting there—nothing appealed to Priyamvad. How could he sit with these cheap people? It occurred to him that amongst the people sitting there some were bound to be labourers from his project. As soon as he realized that he couldn't bear to be there for another second.

He had just come here for a new experience. Maybe he would get to enjoy some good music, a thumri or a *kajri* perhaps. But this place was cheap. And the girls were singing movie songs accompanied by bad musicians.

He got up to leave. As he lifted his head after putting on his shoes, he saw that girl standing there.

The girl looked like she wore a river, her hair was like thick, dark monsoon clouds. Her eyes were like a deep lake, her eyelashes like a gossamer curtain, her kajal like a swaying snake. Seeing her standing so close, and so clearly, Priyamvad suddenly couldn't breathe.

She blocked the doorway with both hands and gestured for him to go back inside. Some spell caused him to follow her back inside and sit down where he had been sitting.

That was that evening three days ago. Three days that seemed like three lifetimes. He didn't want to work. He didn't have the courage to go back there. Society's shackles blocked his way. He had been told about girls like these, and how they were not worthy of love.

Priyamvad sat at the tea stall every day, waiting for Guddu. That day she had asked Priyamvad why he was leaving, and his reply had made her garish red lips widen into a smile.

The tabla player was sprinkling powder on his tabla, the harmonium player indicated a new song. That girl's 'Mausi' had come and sat down beside him. He knew about these Mausis, the owners of these premises and businesses.

With a thoroughly professional smile, Mausi had said, 'Son, there are no appreciators of real music and dance any more. These days everyone wants film songs. Who wants to listen to a traditional courtesan's mujra any more? The people here seek something else, with their lustful needs and eyes.'

Priyamvad appreciated the truth in Mausi's words, there was no artifice. These people had killed art. It was just a business. Whatever the market demanded, the artist provided.

So, that day, that girl, who had introduced herself as Kajal, then Juhi and then Karishma, had sung a kajri for Priyamvad. And when she had sung a Begum Akhtar piece, the pain and honesty in her voice had cleaved through Priyamvad's heart.

Ever since he had left Priyamvad had prayed that he would see her again. Her put-on face had so much honesty, there was such simplicity and beauty behind that garish, cheap make-up.

A sound jerked him out of his reverie. Guddu stood in front of him.

'Guddu! Where had you disappeared?' Priyamvad asked excitedly.

Guddu said nothing but led him purposefully to a dark spot away from the stall. He was limping heavily. 'I had terrible pain in my feet these last two days,' he said. He held his hand and led him to a dark shadow.

'You!' Priyamvad was shocked. 'What should I call you? Juhi, Karishma or Kajal?'

'No, sir, those are all my assumed names. I have come to thank you for that day.'

'Thank me?' Priyamvad was surprised.

'You recognized our art. Only art. You are the first person ever to do that. Anyway, Mausi was remembering you. Do come again.' That girl with many names tried to use Urdu to regain her courtesan's image.

It was business time so she was in a hurry. She said namaste and left. She had barely taken a few steps when she turned around and said, 'And yes, my real name is Gudiya. Gudiya.'

Priyamvad watched her go. He met her many times after that. And watched her from up close: light brown liquid eyes, quivering lips. Every time Priyamvad looked at her, Gudiya would blush with a sweet shyness. When their eyes met, hers would drop of their own volition.

They were not meeting alone, Guddu was with them. As he sat always with her in his arms Priyamvad wished time would stop, the moon would stay where it was, the breeze would be just as it was then. He gently pushed back a strand of hair from her face.

That day she wore no make-up, no powder, no kajal, no lipstick. She was just herself. But this bliss wasn't to last long. Guddu called loudly, 'Kajal, Mausi is calling you. We have an order to dance at a wedding.'

Gudiya had given her cell phone to Guddu and Mausi had just called. After talking to her Guddu came up to Priyamvad. 'Sir, if you don't mind, I'd like to say something. It's not good to fall in love with a courtesan. I took you to watch a dance, but you're now falling in love. Mausi is getting angry.'

And then he left.

Gudiya had said bye and left, promising to come back soon. Priyamvad had asked, 'Do you have to go? Why don't you leave this work?'

Gudiya was in a quandary, she didn't know whether she should say anything or not. She would tell him, but not now. It wasn't good for a relationship to hide the truth, and this was a relationship of the heart.

After all, what was she? A dancing girl from an infamous area. No one considered her profession art; in fact, it was called all kinds of dirty words. Every evening she had to dance in front of an audience; it didn't matter who it was made up of: rich, poor, educated, uneducated, young, old, dirty, clean, handsome, as long they had money in their pockets.

No one knew her name, and no one had looked beyond her false names to see a child, a girl, a woman who could be a daughter, a sister, a mother or a wife.

She knew Priyamvad loved her. She trusted his love. But a man like Priyamvad could never be her future. Nor was she his. He would be able to fight through life without her, but he wouldn't be able to fight with the world and society for her.

Priyamvad was unlike any man she had met.

She had always lived by one principle: dance fully and sing deeply. Ever since she had fallen in love with Priyamvad, after work, she would often sit for hours singing songs of Begum Akhtar in her heart-rending voice.

These Begum Akhtar ghazals would deepen the sadness of her nights. And it got worse the day Guddu lurched around the courtyard singing, 'Bhurey Bhai is coming! Bhurey Bhai is coming!'

Mausi had passed on the information about Gudiya and Priyamvad's love affair to Bhurey Bhai, who was in fact no one's brother. He had taken so many sisters to so many brothels and so denied them all relationships. This was the same Bhurey Bhai, the uncrowned king of the business. It was his law that any girl, under no circumstances, was permitted to fall in love.

And if, heaven forbid, someone was to fall in love, they must never try to run away. They could succumb to their grief and bang their heads against the walls, but they were never to try to break their shackles.

There were shackles on both sides. Priyamvad was shackled. Gudiya was shackled. When Bhurey Bhai arrived he wasted no time in putting a loaded pistol to her head. The feeling of the cold metal sent shivers up her spine.

In his steely voice he had said, 'Look, I'm not your enemy. You go, go and tell that engineer that if he is willing to keep you, then I have no problem. But don't think I am a great friend of yours either, and that I will just let you go to him. I know he is a decent man, he will never be able to convince his family, let alone the society he lives in. Now go!'

Everyone had a good laugh at his words. Mausi laughed too. Clenching her teeth in anger Gudiya went to look for Priyamvad.

Priyamvad had been shocked when Gudiya had walked into his office openly. She had cursed Guddu the whole way there about having told Bhurey Bhai about her love. Guddu swore over and over that it hadn't been him.

Actually it had been Mausi's work. If Gudiya had left what would happen to her business? In his hard hut outside the container that served as his office, Priyamvad was flustered, 'What happened? You, here?'

Gudiya was in a rage. 'Why? Are you feeling bad that a dancing girl has come to your high-class office? Today is the day your love is tested, sir! Let's see what the truth is!'

Guddu had a better understanding of the world. He felt that she should not have come here like that. People like Priyamvad have a standing in society. Priyamvad sat them down and ordered tea. Slowly he understood what had happened. He was up against a challenge, Bhurey Bhai's challenge, Mausi's challenge, the challenge of a whole business, and at stake was Love.

What should he do? Call his mother? Who had already sent him dozens of photographs of educated girls, potential wives whose fathers were engineers, judges, bank managers, all very established. He knew that most of them were buyers in the business, like people buy bulls, gauging the height at the shoulder, touching the horns, checking the shine in the eyes.

'Are you with her?' Priyamvad asked Guddu.

'Yes, sir,' Guddu replied.

'Then come to the station at the time of the six o'clock train,' Priyamvad said and called his mother. Guddu and Gudiya could hear the screams from the other side of the phone.

Guddu stood up, said 'okay' decisively and they left.

'Do you think it is a good idea to go to the station?' he asked finally.

'We'll reach at exactly quarter to six. You'll stay with me?' she asked.

'What do you think? He'll come?'

'This is the test, Guddu, for me as well. Let's see what the truth is.'

The afternoon turned into evening without anyone noticing. But after a quarter to six time began to drag. Every second seemed to ask, will he come?

It was a quarter past six now.

Guddu glanced at Gudiya, 'He won't come now, let's go back.' Gudiya understood. No one came after making promises like that. She was an astute player of the market, how had she fallen for this? Bhurey Bhai had been right.

She still had a half-hearted hope. 'Let's have a cup of tea before we go.'

They had been sitting at the tea shop for an hour and a half and had drunk five glasses of tea. Guddu had given up. Gudiya too had stood up to leave. She turned around to search the darkness one last time, with one last hope in her tear-filled eyes. Priyamvad was running towards them.

'What can I say? I ran to the market straight from office. I got late looking for a ring, I just couldn't find a proper one.'

And then, still panting, at the tea shop, in front of everyone, Priyamvad went down on his knee and said, 'The truth is that I am in love with you. Will you marry me?'

OUR PEOPLE

Kanchan Pant

The sky had cleared after the rain. The night seemed dark and frightening. The neighbourhood slept uneasily under an oppressive silence. The area was littered with smouldering wood and shattered glass and stones, as if left in the wake of a storm. Aarfa had been hiding behind a wall for a while. When she was sure that no one except Gabbar who lay in front of the Community Centre could see her, she left her hiding place. Gabbar came up to her, whining and wagging his tail, expecting a roti from her today too. But she walked away without looking at him, to the last house at the end of a narrow lane. Her eyes had an indescribable emptiness as they looked out from behind the dupatta that veiled her face. A naked bulb shone sadly from a rough wooden pole. In that dim light, Aarfa found her way to the yellow house that until a week ago had been her home. There was a large wooden gate at the front, a twisted iron rod where a lock should have been.

For a moment Aarfa stood confused; she remembered not stopping to lock the gate when she had run out of the house with Ammi and Bhabhi and Sahir. What was the iron rod doing there? She was sure her house had been occupied too. Where did things remain the same after riots? She took a deep breath and, hitching her long kurta up, jumped over the gate. Her heart trembled at the thought of having to sneak into her own house like a thief. What would happen if someone saw her? Shaziya bhabhi had been right—she should not have come. But now she was here. How could she go back without going inside? Her seven-month-old nephew's face flashed across her mind; just a few minutes to retrieve his medicines and then she would sever herself from this house, this neighbourhood, even this city.

She cleared the courtyard in one leap, and then drew up in front of the door. The jasmine tree near it cast a large shadow. For a moment it seemed as if that dark crowd was still gathered there. Fear flooded her veins. She was so scared these days. What a terrible punishment it was to have to be fearful in one's own home. She wished she could say that to the crowd. She calmed herself and pushed the door. It didn't open. Sometimes during the rains, when the wood swelled, it would get stuck. She pulled the left panel towards herself and pushed the right one with her shoulder, and like always it opened. The first voice she always heard when she opened that door was Ammi's.

'How many times have I told you not to push the door like that? Do you people have any sensitivity? And who has come in wearing outdoor slippers?'

And if anyone made the mistake of answering, they had a whole month's worth of complaints to answer for.

'I had asked for that jar from Garima chachi . . . did you get it?'

'And Rafiq, you better stop all this cricket-shicket; I've been asking you for a week now to get that tap fixed. You have time for everything except my work.'

Aarfa and her older brother Rafiq had got used to listening to Ammi and then letting her words loose upon the breeze. And then three years ago Shaziya bhabhi had joined their gang. She was married to Rafiq bhai but she was more like Aarfa's friend and Ammi's daughter than his wife.

'Don't you worry about those two, Ammi, I'll settle them both!' Shaziya bhabhi would say lovingly, handing her a cup of tea, and the two of them would giggle. But today the house was silent. Those voices had been buried there forever.

Aarfa still didn't know how the fire started. Maybe a child's cricket shot had landed in the small temple on the side of the ground. When and how that ball became a stone, and that stone left the temple and entered people's homes, no one knew. That's how riots always started: some people incited and others followed them into the fire. When she had heard about riots in other cities she was always reminded of those sheep in Turkey that followed one another off the cliff to their deaths.

Something very strange had happened the day before. In the relief camp where she now stayed with her family, an NGO had come to distribute aid. Thousands of people stood in line for a few hundred relief packets. Aarfa had gone too, but she had stood on one side. Suddenly it seemed to her as if the people had turned into sheep—big, small, different colours, little lambs in the middle, their voices sounding like senseless bleating. She had held her head. She didn't understand what she was feeling. If someone said she was sad, she felt sad; if someone said she was angry she did feel that she was angry. And if someone asked why she was scared she would think that maybe she wasn't angry at all, just scared.

Was she going mad? After coming to her house today she felt convinced that she was. She pulled herself together and felt her way around the house till she reached the living room. Just then she bumped into the sofa and drew back. That's where Rafiq bhai's body had lain. That day, when the crowd had entered their home, Rafiq bhai had hidden them behind the large chest and gone out saying, 'Don't worry, Ammi, Amit is with them, they won't do anything.' But that day Amit had refused to recognize his opening partner. That day she had learnt that a crowd is just a crowd, there are no people in it, no relationships, no faces, no hearts, no minds. That faceless, nameless crowd had killed her brother right there. Aarfa fell to the ground. How she wished the crowd had killed them all. She was going to cry when she heard a sound from the back door. Frightened, she hid behind the sofa. It was easy to think about dying, but who really wants to die? Those people who were now reduced to numbers in official files hadn't wanted to die. Nor had Rafiq bhai. She bit her dupatta and crouched lower, because two feet were coming in her direction.

Aarfa had been hiding behind the sofa for some ten minutes now. She could still only see the feet of the person who had entered the house. She tried to gauge what he was doing by the sounds he made. The broken glass window let a sliver of moonlight into the room. In its dim light, Aarfa looked around. When the riots had started they had all been sitting in this room, watching TV. *Hum Aapke Hain Koun . . . !* was on; she and Rafiq bhai were fighting over the remote.

'Just change the channel, Aaroo, you've seen this film a hundred times. Don't be annoying,' he had said.

'Close your eyes *na*, if you don't want to watch!' Aarfa had retorted. Ammi had been sitting on the floor shelling peas and Shaziya bhabhi was drinking tea. Just then a stone had come crashing through the window and the glass had scattered around the room.

Ammi had been so angry. 'I'm not going to let them go today. Why can't these rascals go and play somewhere else? Such a big field they have out there.' She went to the window to shout at the children she thought were out playing. But she froze at what she saw.

The scraping of a chair broke Aarfa's reverie. The room was exactly how they had left it. Dried peas were scattered everywhere, the cushion was on the floor and an unfinished cup of tea lay on the table. Ammi couldn't bear a messy house. If she saw her house today she would have yelled at everyone. She realized how much she loved being yelled at by Ammi. She couldn't see but it appeared as if the man was arranging things. She was straining to catch a glimpse when he suddenly bent down to pick up the peas and they found themselves face to face with each other.

'Aaroo?' he asked, shocked. The peas he had picked up fell to the floor again. Aarfa came out from behind the sofa. The person standing before her was Sharad, her neighbour, her childhood friend. Sometimes it seemed as if they were more than friends but the label still read friends. But what was Sharad doing here? At this time of night?

When circumstances change, they sometimes change relationships as well. Until today, Sharad had been Aarfa's friend, someone she took her problems to without thinking twice. But today, when she needed a friend more than ever, she couldn't take a step towards him. He suddenly looked like Amit, and then like the crowd that had killed her brother. His name, Sharad Sharma, stood like a wall before her. Sharad came up to her and, clasping her cold hands, said, 'Thank God you're okay. How is Chachi? And Bhabhi and Sahir? We called your *phuphi* in Kanpur but she said you hadn't gone there. We were so worried.'

Aarfa should have cried when she heard those words. There were very few people left now to worry about her. But she didn't cry. Her heart felt heavier. She slowly drew her hands out of Sharad's and asked, 'So now this house has become yours?'

'When wasn't it my house?' he replied.

He sat her down on the sofa and asked her over and over again if they were okay. He told her about what had happened after they left. She listened in silence as if none of it was about her. She wasn't even sad, just numb. She remembered an evening . . . was it last January? The city had been tense then too. There had been some incidents of arson towards Lalbagh. Aarfa and Sharad had been returning from college when they had been surrounded by four or five men armed with pipes and sticks.

'Name?' one of them had put a stick on Sharad's shoulder and asked. He had stood up cautiously, looking him in the eye, as if trying to determine what name would be safe to give. Aarfa was furious; she wanted to smash the face of that man and scream, *My name is Arti Sharma, kill me now.* But then she remembered Sharad. She needed to control her temper. She said, 'Bhai jaan, my name is Aarfa Javed. Here is my PAN card. This is my husband.' The man looked them over once and said, 'Go straight home. You know how bad the times are.'

Aarfa had wanted to laugh. The people who had ruined the times were complaining! A time when a name was only that—a name. At that moment, Sharad was also just a name for her.

'You stay with us tonight. I'll go and get Chachi and Bhabhi tomorrow,' Sharad said.

'So that your people can kill us all?' Aarfa asked, her tone bitter.

Your people! The words seemed to freeze in Aarfa's mouth. She had lost; the people who had started the fire had won.

A strange silence filled the room. Sharad who had been a friend felt like a criminal. What could he say to someone who had built a wall around herself? The night was deepening, but these days Aarfa felt safer at night than in the day. She went to the cupboard and started looking for Sahir's medicine.

'You're leaving?' Sharad asked as Aarfa headed towards the door. Instead of replying she covered her face with her dupatta and kept walking.

'I'm sorry, Aaroo!' Sharad said. It infuriated Aarfa.

'Why? Why are you sorry? You didn't kill Rafiq bhai.' All her pent-up anger burst forth.

Sharad answered calmly, 'No, I didn't kill him. I'm sorry because I wasn't able to show you that we are your people.'

Aarfa stared at him. Something began to melt inside her. She didn't want to appear weak in front of him so she turned away. She opened the door and stepped out to see a small diya burning at the doorstep.

'It's Chhoti Diwali today. The house shouldn't be dark on Diwali,' Sharad said from behind her. Aarfa stopped where she was. She was a little girl again who had just moved into this locality. It was Diwali. Sharad's mother had just stepped out of their house with a tray full of diyas. Sharad held the corner of her sari. Chachi was decorating her courtyard with lamps, lifting them off the tray one by one. Suddenly she noticed Aarfa. She smiled and Aarfa smiled back. She held one diya out to Aarfa and said, 'The house shouldn't be dark on Diwali.' Since then they had celebrated Diwali together. They never felt that it wasn't their festival. When the joy of lighting the lamps, the fun of making rangolis and the excitement of the fireworks were all hers, why had these people become strangers?

'I'm going,' she said. Sharad's face fell.

She smiled as she turned around, 'How will I bring them back if I don't go?' The weight that had burdened her for days lifted. This house was hers, this neighbourhood was hers, these people were hers. It was election time in the city. Aarfa decided that she would choose love, not hatred. This time and every time.

THE OVERCOAT

Chhavi Nigam

A drowsy morning was rising over Nainital. The streets still slept. A blanket of mist covered the lake and, behind it, the brown tips of the mountain were turning golden in the sun.

Matching my steps to the sounds of the bells from the Naina Devi temple, I marched towards the stadium on the flats. I stopped a chai-wallah for some tea and sat down on the steps. Peace! Apart from the few children skating around there was no one to disturb me.

I smiled as I relished the familiar taste of ginger and cardamom. I thought of my college in Delhi, and of Sashwat. He liked strong black coffee but would always have a sip of my tea that inevitably made him scrunch his face up in distaste. In return I always had a sip of his coffee and pulled an even worse face. Whenever he pushed a plate of sprouts in front of me I would stuff a bread pakora into his mouth.

We were complete opposites. But our friendship was very successful. There were no impositions, no need to change oneself for the other and no expectations whatsoever. We enjoyed being together, and fought a lot, but there was no pressure to make up. It was all going along so well, until he went and spoiled it all the night of the farewell party.

After dancing the salsa for hours, I was exhausted. But after dropping me back to the hostel, Sashwat lingered, refusing to leave. I said bye for the third time and turned to leave. He reached out and held my hand. I had never seen his brown eyes so serious.

'I love you, Saavi,' he said. I was stunned. Then I thought he was joking.

'I'm serious. And I will wait for you forever.'

Brushing him off, I said, 'Oh come on! Don't pull these dialogues on me. 'Love' and 'forever' . . . are they even real?'

But for some reason I couldn't meet his eyes.

Sitting on the steps that cold morning a tremble ran through me as it had when Sashwat had held me close in his arms. I pulled the overcoat tighter around me. I could still hear the words he had whispered, 'I believe in my kind of love. You figure yours out. And I am going to wait for you. The forever kind of waiting.'

I didn't know what to say. From then until I reached Nainital, I had been trying to figure out things, things between Sashwat and me. But in vain.

I stood up, thrusting my hands into the pockets of my overcoat. Just thinking about love was making it all the more complicated.

My footsteps slowed as I climbed the steep hill. It wasn't that I didn't like Sashwat, or that I was interested in a casual relationship—we got on so well together. But it was fine while we were just friends. All this love business, it was beyond me.

I had been in boarding schools all my life; maybe that's why married life didn't appeal to me so much. My parents' lives seemed sad and tedious and Chacha and Chachi's full of arguments and bickering. I doubt Bua had ever been touched by the slightest sensation of love, ever. And Sumit and Kusum's affairs and break-ups seemed like a game to me. What was the point in empty relationships like these?

Sashwat's friendship was the most beautiful thing in my life. I wouldn't hurt him for the world. But how could I accept his proposal when I didn't even believe in love?

Tired, I leant against the trunk of a deodar tree. After a while, as I was starting to walk again I felt something brush against my fingers in one of the coat pockets. Intrigued, I felt around some more. The sewing of the inner lining was coming apart and there seemed to be things within. I pulled them out one by one and sat down on the grass to inspect the objects now spread on my lap.

There were some coins, a button, a refill, a handkerchief and a crumpled, fraying piece of paper and a ring. As I straightened out the sheet I realized it was a letter. I tried to read the words. It was a poem by Shakespeare: 'True Love'. There were more words underneath, but the letter was so stained that I struggled to make sense of the writing.

Love you . . . shall wait forever . . . yours, P.

The words sounded familiar. They reminded me of Sashwat. Hadn't he said the same things to me?

But this letter had been written by some P! To whom? What love was this about? Who was waiting forever? Waiting for whom? Whose tears had smudged the words?

My mind raced as I held the ring and the letter in my hand. Maybe solving this mystery would help me find a solution; this thought took hold of my mind.

I sat there for a while. A cold wind pushed against me, I pulled the overcoat tighter. This is how relationships should be, big enough to give you space, and there to hold you in a warm embrace when you needed it. Oh and pockets for the bits and pieces of feelings! But love can't be like that. What use was a love that made you weak? The letter fluttered in the breeze. The letter and the other things must belong to the prior owner of the overcoat. Who could it have been?

I tried to remember.

When I had reached last night, everyone else was already there. While we ate there was the usual conversation and I had tried to dodge the usual questions that were always directed at me. I had tossed and turned the whole night wondering what to say to Sashwat. In the morning when I set out, I had found the coat hanging on the stand and had slipped into it. The coat could be anyone's, and the letter?

Papa and Mummy would never write a letter like that to each other. That a third person would have written it to either was too far-fetched. Then there was Bua. With her hair always in a tight bun, Bua was as stiff and stern as her starched saris. She taught in a school. She lived in the corner-most room of the large house. You only approached Bua if you were desperate. Who would invite total destruction by writing a letter like that to her?

Next on my list of suspects were Chacha and Chachi. They had had a love marriage so they were the more likely candidates. But still it seemed unlikely. I was willing to bet anything Chacha didn't even know that Chachi liked *gajra*s. And I'm sure Chachi had no interest in Chacha's obsession with Talat Mehmood. A third person? Impossible.

That left me with Chacha and Chachi's children, Sumit and Kusum. They were the WhatsApp and Facebook generation; why would they write a letter like that to anyone? And it was even more unlikely that anyone would write to them.

So did the coat belong to some other relative? Or a guest? That would make my investigation even harder.

On the walk back I decided that I would hang the coat on the stand and just wait to see who would claim it. I had come here to try and solve the Sashwat mystery but I was getting even more caught up in a whole other case.

They were all up by the time I reached home and soon the kitchen was redolent with all the cooking. Sumit and Kusum wanted all my Delhi news, Papa and Chacha had gone down to the bazaar to buy things I liked to eat. Mummy was oiling my hair and Chachi was going through the magazines I had brought up with me. Bua had come up to the room a few times and, after hesitating at the door, had gone back. I only concentrated on that coat.

Finally late in the evening I saw someone take the overcoat off the stand and put it on. I was astounded! It was Bua! She was now going down the stairs and out of the house wearing the coat!

'Bua?'

I said it out loud as if to convince myself that I had really seen her. How was it possible? I was finding it hard to believe that someone could be in love with her, write letters like that to her. And Bua? Did she love him too?

For a while I stood there stunned. Then as the disbelief died, I realized how little I actually knew Bua. It wasn't just me; no one in the house knew her at all.

I remembered that when I was a child, Bua had been the only person who would give me a doll or a dress for my birthday, unlike everyone else who got me boxes of biscuits.

And when I fooled around instead of studying, she would pull my ears really hard. I remember the perfume that came from her bag full of books as I walked holding her finger on the long, winding road to school.

Bua had been the most intelligent person in our entire joint family, which often earned her Baba's praise. 'This is my most clever son!' he would say proudly. And like a reliable son, slowly she had started taking over the responsibility of the whole household. She had forgotten about herself and her own dreams. All the marriages, everyone's education, she had taken care of everything. No one noticed when the love they must have once felt for her turned into respect.

Now when I thought about it, I realized that she had smothered her youth with her sense of duty. How did it happen that everyone got so caught up in their lives that they forgot all about her? Why had she become so grown up that no one thought to take some responsibility for her?

Despite all this, in all my memories she smiled—that lovely smile that always lit up her eyes. And there was peace. In all those years I had never seen her angry or miserable.

Suddenly, I felt like going to her room.

The gallery across Bua's room was darkening with the evening's shadows. I couldn't remember the last time I had gone to this part of the house. I only messaged her a thank you when I received the cheques she sent. And whenever I came home, if she saw me, she would ask, 'How are you, Saavi?' and I would say, 'I'm fine,' and turn to all the other people in the house. But today I wanted to see her through new eyes.

As I neared her door, to my amazement, I heard her humming. 'Bua?' I called out softly.

There was silence and then, with halting words, she said, 'Is that you, Saavi? Come inside.'

I went in and found that I couldn't take my eyes off her. She looked completely different in a blue nightgown. There was something different about her face, a kind of peacefulness that glowed. She looked lovely.

Undoing her bun, she asked, 'Did you want something?'

I tore my gaze from her cascading hair with difficulty and found myself looking at her eyes, unhidden behind glasses for the first time. They reminded me of thick deodars and blue clouds. A light shone in them. She asked again and I hesitated before replying, 'No, I just wanted to meet you.'

I think it may have been the first time someone had come just to see her. A few tears slipped from her eyes, caressing me as they fell.

Under that demeanour of authority, how alone she really was! Tied down by her responsibilities. But still something had soothed that loneliness inside her. You could tell from the peace she exuded, from her smile that never faded.

Slowly I began to understand. After finding the letter I understood her love for life. That thing we call love, that was the light that lit up her face. The words in that letter must be giving her courage. Despite her not committing to him, there was still someone waiting for her. Perhaps the calmness which came with knowing that was enough to live by.

Something began to melt inside me. Is this the love that is enough to live your life by? Was this the waiting that Sashwat was willing to do for me? Through the tears that were filling my eyes I tried to understand this nameless bond.

As I looked around her room through blurry eyes I noticed a beautiful card peeping out from behind her medals and books. I stood up. This time it was a poem by William Wordsworth. I wiped my eyes and read the name of the sender: Prashant.

A memory suddenly flooded my mind. As I had held Bua's finger and walked to school a person would join us somewhere along the way and walk with us. I had seen them look at each other and smile sometimes. Often he would recite poems as we walked. For Bua?

Then suddenly I remembered his name. My jaw dropped.

'This is the English teacher, isn't it? Prashant sir?'

I turned to look at Bua. She was blushing. I could read her now. I could see the love on her face. I didn't need to ask any questions. Smiling, I left the room.

It was dark now and Nainital twinkled in the night. It was getting cold so I put on a blue overcoat I found hanging on the stand and made my way down to Tallital. The boats glimmered like fireflies. The sound of the temple bells wafting in the breeze filled me with its serenity.

In the course of that one day, I had grown up. I had learned something. A letter had taught me about love. A beautiful relationship had shown me how to understand all relationships a little better.

After discovering Bua and Prashant sir's love, love was no more just a word in a cheesy dialogue. It was real. It made me want to risk a forever like theirs.

I wanted to talk to Sashwat. I decided that I would speak to him that very night. I felt at ease, content.

A cold gust of wind teased me as it passed by. I pulled the overcoat around me tightly and slipped my hands into the pockets. The lining of this one was torn too! Now what secret was this blue overcoat waiting to unfold?

TOGETHER

Jamshed Qamar Siddiqui

Abba would tell me of my grandfather, a lawyer in Lahore, and how strict he was about his morning walks. That was before the Partition. My father had inherited this habit from him. I'm old now but I do have faint memories of when we first shifted to Delhi after the Partition, and Abba would ask me to accompany him. But nothing would induce me to get out of bed until nine.

An age has passed since then, and now, in my retirement, when I walk slowly from my apartment in the haze of the early morning, I miss Abba. I miss Rehana, my wife. She had died of hepatitis a few years before I retired.

It was on my morning walks after Rehana's death that I realized how important a companion is at this stage in life. The stage when the life you built so conscientiously starts to stare back at you, your body begins to abandon you and your children become impatient. I was at this age. I missed Rehana so much, her beautiful smiling face, the mole on her wrist, her heavy-framed glasses which were my responsibility to keep clean. Even in the middle of a fight she would suddenly hand me her glasses and I would carefully wipe them on the sleeve of my shirt and hand them back to her. For those few minutes hostilities would cease. Then as she put the glasses back on she would say, 'Haan, what were you saying?'

When Rehana died I had wanted to leave my job at the bank. But my son, Zaheer, advised me not to. 'Abba I think it will be better for you to work, it will keep your mind occupied,' he had said. I had changed my mind then, but sooner or later I had to retire. And now, in my retirement, I felt a strange emptiness. I won't call it loneliness, I was not alone. My son, his Romanian wife, Aliyana, and my grandson, Amaan, lived with me in my Vasant Kunj flat. There were people around me, but nobody with me.

But I had my walks.

There was a park not far from my apartment block. I walked there twice a day, morning and evening. I spent more time there than at home. So much so that I could tell you exactly how many eucalyptus trees there were, and which spot on which particular bench caught the best breeze, and who came to the park at what time. The park had lots of regulars. I knew all the faces. Lately, though, I had become aware of a new face.

A woman, ageing, her greying hair suggesting that she was probably a few years younger than me. She always sat on the yellow bench in the far corner of the park. Once, as I walked past, I saw that she was reading a book, reading as if she were drowning in it. 'May I sit here?' I asked hesitantly one day. She lifted her head and peered at me through her glasses. 'Yes?' she asked, surprised. 'If you don't mind, may I sit here?' I asked again. She quickly glanced at the other benches in the park, they were all full. 'Of course,' she said, 'why not?' and shifted over to one end of the bench and started reading again. And I began to read her.

As she read her face would suddenly become sad, sometimes a faint laugh would light it up, sometimes a faint worry would furrow her eyebrows, sometimes peace would settle on it. Her expressions reflected whatever she read. I watched her. After a couple of hours she closed the book and put it into her bag, stood up with some difficulty (her knees troubled her perhaps) and then slowly walked towards the main gate.

This went on for some days. She would walk to the yellow bench, read for a few hours and then leave. I had never, in all my hours in the park, found the peace that she seemed to find in her book.

'If you don't mind, may I ask you something? What is it that you read so intently?' I mustered up the courage to ask one day. She smiled and replied, 'Amrita. Have you heard of her? Amrita Pritam?' I shook my head. 'She writes beautifully, I'm reading a book by her.'

'You?' she inquired. 'I live close by,' I replied, 'But I spend most of my time in this park. I'm a retired bank officer.' She smiled. Her smile pulled at her wrinkles, deepening them. 'You seem to have some trouble with your knees,' I said. She closed the book and looked straight at me and said, 'Yes, at this age it's the knees that hurt, the heart is beyond all that.' We both had a laugh.

That was our first proper meeting. We spent time together after that, getting to know each other. I seemed to be alive again. Vrinda and I had found a friend in each other.

Our friendship grew. It had the wonderful informality that friendship should have. Vrinda's story was similar to mine. After the death of her husband, she too was trying to cope with the aloneness that age and circumstances brought with them. She had found a way to deal with it through books. She read Amrita Pritam's autobiography, *Raseedi Ticket*, to me. Once she said, 'Amrita lived with Imroz but she loved Sahir just as much. She and Sahir never got together though . . . You know Sahir? Sahir Ludhianvi?' I didn't know much about him but at least I knew who he was, so I nodded. She went on to tell me how sometimes, when Amrita and Imroz were riding on his scooter, Amrita would trace Sahir's name on Imroz's back. She told me many more entrancing stories and anecdotes. When she asked me to tell her something it almost always began with, 'One day at the bank . . .' and she would say, 'Please, not about work, tell me something else instead.' And I would get annoyed and say, 'What should I talk about then? I don't read interesting books.' And she would say, 'Tell me about Rehana.'

That was a deep question. I think the detail with which I answered that took Vrinda by surprise. But I talked and she listened. I remembered every tiny detail: our arranged marriage in Delhi, our first holiday together in Mussoorie, she had gifted me a striped sweater and I had given her a pair of silver anklets, my first gift to her. She had worn those anklets her whole life. In fact, a few days before she died, in the hospital, she had said, 'Bury these anklets with me.' And I had put my hands to her lips to stop her words, saying, 'Nothing will happen to you.' I remembered everything about Rehana, every wrinkle, the lines on her face, the mole on her wrist, her palms, old and rough, that she had laid gently on my face, a few hours before she died.

'You're crying!' as I looked up at Vrinda and exclaimed as she wiped her wet eyes. We were both late going home that day. When I reached home, Zaheer was furious. I think he and Aliyana had been looking for me for a while.

'Is this any time to come home, Abba? After a long day at work, I want to rest, not run around looking for you,' Zaheer's voice was thick with anger. Aliyana spoke from behind him, 'We were looking all over for you. Do you have any idea how worried we were? Not fair.' She flounced away, sweeping a bewildered Amaan away with her as she left. Zaheer came up to me and said, 'You shouldn't go out without telling us. Look at how upset Aliyana is.'

The house was quiet that night. I went into my room and lay down. At ten o'clock that night there was a sound at my door. It was Amaan; he had a torch in his hand. He often came to my room at night like that. When his parents were asleep he would creep into my room with his torch and snuggle up under my razai with me. We would whisper like secret agents in the torchlight.

He lit the torch under the razai and asked, 'Dada, had you gone away somewhere? Papa was very angry.' 'Yes,' I said, 'but I had some very important work.' And then changing the subject I asked, 'Have you seen the new nest on the roof? Has it hatched yet?' He was quiet and then asked, 'You must have felt really bad when Papa spoke to you like that?' The innocence of that question deepened the silence of the night. 'Not at all,' I said, 'he was only angry because he was worried. And that's because he loves me very much. Do you understand?'

I don't know what Amaan made of that explanation. For a long time after he went, a memory played in my head, an incident from a long time ago. Zaheer was a small boy. One day, instead of coming home from school, he and his friends had gone straight to a video parlour. Rehana and I had waited for him for quite a while. Then in a panic, we ran to school and he wasn't there. Desperate, we looked for him everywhere. We had been worried too, we loved him too. But when we finally found him we didn't scream at him. We had just held him tight, to our hearts. Maybe there is a difference in the way parents love their children and children their parents.

The next morning was a special one. Vrinda and I were going to a cafe together for the first time. I had made special arrangements. I had ordered a special sugar-free cake for us. It said: 'Cheers to our friendship!'

The air in the cafe was rich with the aroma of coffee; the sound of customers talking, and of their chairs as they arrived and left, filled the room. In one corner at a table set against a large window, Vrinda and I sat across from each other. She looked lovely that day. Her skin was old now, loose around her neck—it looked beautiful to me. The wrinkles were poetry on her face, a nazm written by her beloved Sahir. Age made her hands shake a little. I felt some music might arise from them as they trembled. We gazed at each other through fading eyes. 'Would you like to order something, sir?' a waiter asked. I ordered two coffees. We talked about everything over coffee: our homes, our families, the people we had lost and our friendship. We cut the cake and shared it with everyone in the cafe.

That was the first official day of our friendship but something also changed that day. We became more than friends. We spent all our time together. She would read to me the love stories of Amrita Pritam and Sahir. And when her glasses got dusty, she would hold them out to me with a smile. I would clean them on the corner of my sleeve. I felt I was listening to a story I had heard before.

Maybe at this stage in life one needs a companion more than a friend. We now wanted to spend all our time together. We wanted to look after each other, to know more about each other. We wanted to spend the rest of our lives being happy. Together.

We didn't have much time to think. We wanted to do what we wanted to do today. Who had seen tomorrow? One evening I said, 'Vrinda, I can't go down on my knees, so I'll have to ask you like this. Will you be mine?' She looked intently at me through her glasses. She knew what I was asking of her was not going to be easy. 'You can trace

Sahir's name on my back,' I said. She smiled and placed her slightly shaking hand in mine.

We had chosen to be happy. But it was against the norm of the times. When I told my son it was as if an earthquake had struck. Society, relatives, people, what will they think, and a host of other opinions ricocheted off the wall and echoed in the house.

'But this is not right! People will laugh at us, Abba!' Zaheer shouted at me. I looked back at him, 'What have I done?' He ranted on, 'What are you punishing me for?' Then drawing close to me he said, 'Are you doing this because you want to shame us into leaving your flat?' Stepping back he said, 'There was no need for you to do all this, we'll leave anyway. As soon as possible.' And he turned and left.

That night was very long. Under my pillow wrapped in paper was a single anklet. I took it out. Tears filled my eyes and flowed down my cheeks. *Please forgive me, Rehana. I didn't fulfil your wish. I buried you with only one anklet. But this anklet is what has kept me alive.* I held it for a while, caressing it.

At four thirty the next morning, the alarm rang as usual. But it was not a usual day. I glanced out of the window. The sun was getting ready to rise, the birds were waking up. Everything was new, as if it had been made just today. As if it was the first day of a new world, and I was the first person to see it.

An hour and a half later, I left the apartment as I had every day. But today I had a bag. I was setting off on a new journey. At the corner of the park, Vrinda was waiting for me. The world looked so beautiful. We boarded the seven-thirty bus to Mussoorie. As I looked out from the window at Delhi falling away in the distance, I thought Zaheer must have read the note I had left him by now.

Zaheer, no, I don't want you to leave. I am going instead. You won't need to answer any questions. But don't forget, son, that when you had brought Aliyana home, from another country, another religion, another culture, the same questions had been before me. What will people say? What will people think? But I had done what I knew would make you happy. But please, don't have regrets. I will come sometimes to visit Amaan when I miss him too much. Be happy, son.

That evening, surrounded by mountains, Vrinda and I sat in a lovely cafe on the Mussoorie Mall Road. She looked lovely, and even more lovely was Rehana's anklet, shining on her foot.

AMAYA

Anulata Raj Nair

As the train roared along the tracks, trees and mountains fell swiftly behind. So did Amaya's past.

Resting her head against the windowpane, she gazed at the moon that was travelling alongside her—it was her only companion now. Perhaps it was companion to every lone traveller setting out on a cheerless journey. Amaya began to see Prashant in the moon, she saw his smiling face.

He had always teased her about her obsession with the moon. 'You should have married a poet, not a gun-toting soldier like me. Then he would have written poems about the moon for you and you would have been happy.' And smiling as she rested her head on his shoulder she had said, 'I'm happy, Prashant. Very happy.'

It was true that he didn't write poems about the moon. In fact, he often called it barren and rocky. He would say, 'Even the moonlight of this moon of yours is borrowed.' But she was very happy with him.

When she was in his arms she felt no pain in the world could touch her. Life was so carefree when he was with her.

The four years after their marriage were the happiest years of her life. They hadn't spent one day apart from each other. They lived fully. He took such good care of her, of her happiness, giving in to every demand she made, whether it was justifiable or not.

Amaya remembered when they had gone to stay at his parents' house for the first time. He would come to check on her every few minutes, to see if she was okay. Sometimes his mother would reprimand her, 'Bahu, don't laugh and joke like that with him in front of people.' She put small restrictions on her like 'walk slowly', 'wear saris'.

One day Prashant had taken her on, 'Ma, why are you insisting? Let her do what she wants!'

Amaya had rebuked him. She had listened to Ma and had gone in and changed into a sari. There was no harm in doing things that made Ma happy while they were there. In a family, if you held yourself in a bit in one aspect you would find the freedom to fly in another.

But Prashant wasn't with her today. He had left her and gone forever. And she, of her own volition, was going back to his home town, to spend the rest of her life there, alone, without him.

She had taken this decision after a lot of thought. She felt that perhaps this is what Prashant would have wanted. And now that he wasn't here any more she had set off to be Prashant.

Tears rolled down her face. She felt as if the past wasn't getting left behind. It was running alongside the train, holding on to the moon's fingers.

The first day at her in-laws' house was very difficult for her. It was the first time she had come here since Prashant's death, and everything had changed.

She was surrounded by mourners the whole day. Some would hug her and weep, others would bemoan her fate. She wished they would leave her alone. She wanted to indulge her grief herself, but perhaps this was society's way, to pick at wounds.

The Amaya who had lived her own life on her own terms had come back to become a part of this same society.

After a few days people stopped coming to the house and Amaya tried to fit into the new house and atmosphere. She started to arrange the things she had brought with her in her room—the room where Prashant had spent his childhood.

There was a black-and-white photograph on the wall in which he held a mike as he sang on the stage in school. Amaya hung another photograph next to it. Prashant held a mike and was singing in this one too. But in this he was singing for her as she sat in the audience.

She smiled. That life-filled photograph eased her pain a little.

It was during those days that Amaya realized that Prashant hadn't left her; he was a part of her. She was pregnant.

She couldn't sleep that night. She sat in the courtyard and looked at the star-filled sky. She wanted to be a child and believe that everyone became a star after they died.

She looked for one that looked familiar.

Every happiness felt incomplete unless she shared it with Prashant. And this was happiness given by Prashant. The next morning she told her mother-in-law about it. Her parched, dry face looked as if someone had sprinkled it with fresh dew. That was the first day she blessed Amaya.

Amaya began to string together the scattered beads of her life into making new bonds. She sang sweet lullabies as she prepared for the beautiful days ahead.

One day Amaya was settling her cupboard. It was a task she loved doing and she did over and over again. The creases in the clothes held memories. A particular fragrance lingered in them. She pulled out a bright orange sari.

Whenever she wore that sari Prashant had said she looked like the setting sun, and she would get annoyed and say, 'At least say rising sun, which had a day to live. Why setting sun that will die in a few minutes?'

Prashant always laughed at her poetic turns and for the thousandth time said, 'You really should have fallen in love with a poet!'

Two drops fell on the sari in her lap.

She draped the bright orange sari about her and stood in front of the mirror. It was evening. She looked out. The setting sun peeped out from behind the pipal tree, exactly the colour of the sari.

The next morning when she wore the orange sari and stepped out of her room, she noticed the questioning looks from the family.

'What's wrong, Ma? Why is everyone looking at me like that?' she asked, puzzled.

After a few minutes her mother-in-law said, 'Does it look nice to wear these bright colours?' Her voice had a hint of censure.

'Why, Ma? This is Prashant's favourite sari,' Amaya answered naively.

Prashant's elder sister replied, 'It was Prashant's favourite, right? Well he's not sitting here now to appreciate you in it.'

Amaya was stunned. The harsh words made her throat dry. She was troubled and went back into her room, without a word.

For the next few days Amaya was told about the colours she could wear and the ones she couldn't. Certainly not Prashant's choice or hers.

Amaya, who had worn the colours of the rainbow, now only had a few colours to choose from: white, brown, blue or grey. This was society's dress code.

She wasn't able to understand what was right and what was wrong. Lying awake till late at night she would wonder, could Ma and Dadi be right? She couldn't understand how dull colours would ease her pain. Would the way she lived now determine whether she loved Prashant or not?

She was getting trapped in her confusion.

Maybe it's true, she thought, when there was nobody to appreciate how she looked any more, how did it matter if she wore brown or white? Dadi wore those colours too.

She sat at her cupboard again. She sorted all the colourful clothes out and put them aside. She was trying to do everything she could to deal with her grief but no one in the house helped her. No one held her hand through the dark nights and led her towards the light of day.

It almost felt as if they didn't want her to be happy. They seemed to have heaped endless mourning on her. The fragrance-filled blossoms she had inside seemed to be drying, as if weeds had taken their place and were spreading roots, taking over everything.

She wanted to uproot them and discard them but the people around her watered and tended to those thorny growths.

She was lonely amongst all those people. She looked for herself in the drab colour draped woman she had become, and got lost again.

The orchard outside the house, full of flowers and fruit, was Amaya's favourite place. Whenever she missed Prashant she would sit in the thick shade of the mango tree, where the previous summer she had scratched a heart and written 'Prashant' inside it. He had scratched a heart and drawn a sun in it. A setting sun.

One morning she had come early to the orchard for a walk. Ma was there collecting fresh flowers. Amaya plucked flowers and began to put them in Ma's thali. Ma looked at her intently. Amaya smiled, but Ma didn't return her smile.

A little later, Ma entered her room with a garland made from the flowers Amaya had chosen and draped it on Prashant's photograph.

Amaya was stunned. 'Why, Ma? I don't like to put flowers on Prashant's photograph,' she said plaintively.

'Why?' Ma asked coldly, her normally calm face ablaze.

'Because they remind me that Prashant isn't alive,' Amaya answered, her voice shaking.

'So? It's true. He isn't.' Ma's words were cold.

Amaya was shocked. Why was Ma being so harsh? She knew Ma felt the pain of Prashant's passing as acutely as she did. But perhaps Ma hadn't understood that.

Thoughts crowded Amaya's mind. Sometimes she remembered the past and sometimes thoughts of the future worried her.

And then the day came when Amaya smiled, from the heart, after ages. Wrapped in pink cotton her tiny daughter lay beside her. Amaya lifted her up and held her to her heart, slipping her finger into her daughter's tiny fist. The baby clenched her fingers. This was her first gesture of trust towards her mother.

After the arrival of her daughter Amaya spent all her time looking after her. She was busy with her own things.

One afternoon as she sang her baby to sleep, she heard Prashant's mother call out loudly, 'Amaya! Amaya!'

She put the baby down in her cot and ran out of her room.

Her mother-in-law and Dadi stood outside her door. She couldn't read the expression on their faces.

'You're singing so loudly the people on the road can hear you. Is it nice to sing these film songs?' Ma asked.

What was wrong with that? Amaya was amazed. Prashant's brother listened to music on full volume the whole day, and sang loudly. But she couldn't say anything.

Just then the baby started crying and after a few moments of standing there, Ma turned and went back to her own room.

For the last seven or eight months Amaya had been observing her mother-in-law's attitude towards her. It was if she, Amaya, was a stranger. She didn't understand what she said, but she did understand what she didn't say.

Amaya's daughter was growing and so were Amaya's responsibilities. Despite the family's interferences she was trying to be a strong person and a good mother.

There were so many restrictions on her. If she resisted, she got trouble. If she agreed quietly, everyone behaved well with her. It was exactly as if a caged bird was being congratulated for clipping its own wings.

Amaya's innocent mind was breaking. The shackles of tradition were beginning to chafe. She was becoming increasingly restless.

One day her daughter saw someone drive past in a scooter and asked for a ride. Her eyes filled with tears.

'Okay! Is this anything to cry about? Come on, we'll go for a ride too.' And Amaya started the scooter parked in the courtyard and took her daughter for a ride. After a few rounds of the block, they came back to find the entire family gathered in the door, their faces furious.

'You have disgraced us in front of the whole society. The next time you go somewhere, take someone with you. And go in a rickshaw,' Ma blazed at her.

Amaya stood at the doorway for a long time. The house seemed like a cage to her. And Ma like a jailer.

Her frightened daughter held her hand tightly and looked from her mother's face to her grandmother's. Amaya's pain was giving way to anger. She understood that her clothes, her driving and everything else aside, she was not permitted to feel happy even during festivals.

It was the monsoon and swings were hung from the mango tree. The same tree that she had carved Prashant's name on. Women would be invited from all around to swing on it. Amaya was always kept away from it. She wasn't permitted to put mehndi on her hands, or wear bangles; she wasn't even allowed to touch them.

Amaya held her daughter's hand and went and sat on the swing, the little girl laughed with joy. Slowly she kicked with her feet and soon the swing was swinging high. Amaya felt she could touch the sky. Just then, her mother-in-law grabbed the rope and jerked the swing to a halt.

She had no right to fly.

That night Amaya couldn't sleep. She couldn't get the picture of her sobbing daughter out of her mind. Her voice was an ache in her ears, 'Ma, I want to swing! Ma, I want to swing!'

Amaya was scared.

The next morning, when Amaya stepped out of her room, she wore the orange sari, Prashant's favourite. The one she had been denied the right to wear. Before anyone could speak she said, 'Ma, I am going to Delhi. I have a job as a teacher in a school there. The pay is good and they are giving me a house to stay in.'

Ma threw the mouthful of food in her hand down on her plate.

Without stopping Amaya continued, 'Ma, I don't want to be a weak woman in front of my daughter. If I keep killing my dreams and wishes, who will keep hers alive? Prashant would never have wanted me to be sad. To be weak. He loved this Amaya, Ma, the Amaya filled with colours. The Amaya who was full of life.'

The family was stunned into silence. They had never seen Amaya like this before.

Amaya spoke again, 'Wherever I stay, Ma, your relationship with this child will never change. I only want that when she and I swing together, no one should be able to hold the rope, and that she can laugh and say, "Higher, Ma! Higher!"'

EVENING TEA

Chhavi Nigam

Ammaji rubbed the lens of her glasses with the edge of her sari for the tenth time, and stared intently at the clock on the wall for perhaps the eleventh time. This was too much. It was five minutes past five and her daughter-in-law still hadn't brought her tea.

Holding on to her knee gently, she got up and went out of her room to the veranda. In the fading sunlight she saw her loneliness and her own declining age. Despite the odd wrinkle she still had a lovely pink blush on her skin. You felt like you should lay your head in her lap and fall asleep listening to a really good story.

Even though her house was small, it used to be filled with people and light and noise. With her shy nature, she had found it hard to deal with Monu's laughter and Babuji's guffaws. Then Monu got married. The first floor was built. And then after her grandson Ashu was born, Monu (or Manish) and his wife Nandini shifted upstairs. After Monu's father had died, they had tried hard to convince her to move upstairs, but she had preferred to stay downstairs. This was where her memories of Monu's father lived. In any case, she was no longer capable of going up and down the stairs. And she was a little apprehensive of what her daughter-in-law might and might not like. She didn't know whether it was consideration for the relationship or a generation gap, or whether they had made no attempt to get to know each other more. But now, they both lived in their own worlds. She was good, her daughter-in-law. And she took care of her. That is why she wondered why Nandini still hadn't brought her tea. Perhaps she was on her way down.

She sat down in the easy chair on the veranda and gently rocked back and forth. An old memory came to caress her half-closed eyes. She was young, the ride in the horse carriage had felt like this rocking, hadn't it? She remembered that day when, stuffed into a horse carriage, she and her whole family had gone to the cinema to watch a film for the first time. The day she had lost her heart to Dev Anand. For her, the most romantic scene in the black-and-white movie had been the one where the hero comes home from office and the heroine—her hair tied up in a high bun, long lines of kajal in her eyes—opens the door and then lifts a beautifully embroidered tea cosy to pour out two cups of tea. Then they proceed to drink their evening tea looking deep into each other's eyes. The tender age that she was at then, this was her first romantic dream.

Ammaji opened her eyes and took a deep breath. She looked at the time. Five-thirty!

The pinkness of her face started to flush a deeper red. A vein on her neck stood out. Is this what she was reduced to in her own house now? Was she, like all the extra furniture downstairs, becoming redundant, unneeded?

Just then the upstairs door opened. Her eyes flared for a minute and then gently closed. It was her grandson Ashu coming down the stairs, not Nandini. Something unpleasant stuck in her throat. It wasn't only a question of drinking tea. The evening tea was a symbol of her status in the house, her relevance. Was Nandini sidelining her? Did she no longer have any place in her heart for her wishes? But why?

Ammaji tried to understand the reasons. She never interfered in her household anyway. Nor did she scold or demand anything. She only wanted her evening tea-time ritual to remain unchanged. In fact at the time of the *muh dikhayi* she had given Nandini an expensive seven-strand gold necklace and stressed that fact. And when smilingly, Nandini had bent down to touch her feet, Ammaji had blessed her. In the beginning everything was okay. But ever since her husband had died, the evening tea was getting delayed further and further. And today it had really crossed the limit.

'Ashu beta, carefully!' Ammaji called to him as she heard him leaping down the stairs.

'Don't worry, dadi,' Ashu said as he kicked the football in his hands crashing it into the gate.

'Okay. What is mummy doing?' she finally asked.

'I don't know. Something on the laptop.' Ashu shrugged his shoulders carelessly and ran off. Ammaji was left staring at the gate from where he had left.

So! Nandini's work had become so important that she had forgotten her mother-in-law? Or was she deliberately ignoring her? She hardly came downstairs. She probably found it hard to bear the time Monu and Ashu spent downstairs too! She tried to remember the time when Nandini had been happy to spend hours sitting with her. The only time she had sat downstairs recently was when she had been here for two hours because she had seen a mouse upstairs. Who is scared of mice? All drama!

It was just she who tolerated everything. Her own mother-in-law had been so strict. But Ammaji had always respected her. In her moments of hopelessness her mother-in-law's face came before her eyes. Dusky, very thin, with a hard voice, was how she had been. She had been the sole ruler of the house. And delicate, innocent Ammaji, laden with golden saris and jewellery as a new bride, had spun around the house on her orders like a Catherine wheel. She woke up at four every morning. She would bathe and prepare her mother-in-law's puja thali, then she would prepare her fruit, then massage her head and comb and plait her hair. She would wash her clothes, look after the cooking and then, late at night, fall into a dead sleep while massaging her mother-in-law's feet. That was how her days had been. Her husband was a lawyer and would keep trying to devise schemes to call her to him on some pretext or the other. But far from meeting, they barely got time to talk to each other.

But eventually, after years of devotion, her mother-in-law had melted. Then, in her naivety, she had told her about her filmi dream. Her mother-in-law had laughed loudly.

But the very next evening, the lawyer and a tea tray with two cups and tea pot under a beautiful tea cosy were sent to her room. That was the most precious gift her mother-in-law had given her. A sweet hesitation, shy eyes slightly lowered, a faint smile, the lightest touch as she handed him his cup. With those sips of tea, Ammaji and Babuji had woven a new relationship.

The evening deepened. She still sat on her easy chair. Through tired eyes she watched the birds hopping about and the squirrels scuttling around, and that naughty mouse that came regularly for the biscuit crumbs she put out for it. She was deep in thought, wondering why she hadn't been able to connect with Nandini despite giving her love. She had never to come to share the loneliness Ammaji experienced after the death of Monu's Babuji.

It was night when Monu came home from office. He sat with her for a while. Ammaji didn't mention the tea incident. She didn't like to cause trouble. And truthfully, the things that hurt our hearts the most are the hardest to talk about. Monu was in a hurry himself. He had to leave the next morning for a week-long office trip. She sent a message through him that she didn't want dinner that night.

The night wore on. When she got fed up of tossing and turning, she sat up. She turned on the light and went into another room. The room was filled with her things: an old sofa, a dressing table, a carved cupboard, big brass pots, trays and all sorts of other objects. No one used these things any more, but her memories were tied up with them. She had kept them all safe.

She struggled with the carved cupboard for a while and then managed to pull out an old photo album, wrapped neatly in an old tablecloth. She dusted it and sat on her bed. Then she opened the album on her lap. With damp eyes she turned the pages. She stopped at a fading black-and-white photograph. She closed her eyes and, sighing deeply, caressed it. In the crystal-clear mirror of her memories, she could see the day her husband had managed to spirit her away from his mother's gaze to the Kartik mela to have a photograph taken. And when they had both stood behind the wooden moon prop for the photo, that idiotic bearded photographer had said coaxingly, 'Arre, stand a little closer! Bhabhiji, move the palla from your head! Now stare into each other's eyes!' Ammaji felt shy just remembering the incident. She turned the page.

In another photograph, her smiling mother-in-law blessed her, her hand gentle on her head. It had been Ammaji's strength that had won her mother-in-law's love. She felt her mother-in-law's hand on her head again. As long as we hold them captive in our memories, our loved ones can't really escape, can they? While her mother-in-law and Babuji had been with her, no one had been able to challenge Ammaji's significance.

When she finally lay down, a slight smile lit her lips. It was a hint of that same determination. Her eyes had the contentment of having taken a decision.

When Monu came to touch Ammaji's feet before leaving the next day, she had already finished her puja. Nandini was probably working at her designing course, she thought as she watered the plants. When she had asked Ammaji's permission to complete the course (that she had left halfway when she got married), Ammaji had given it happily. She remembered her own experience. She had decided that when she became a mother-in-law, she would never impose her will on her daughter-in-law. So that her respect would be born out of love, not fear. But now . . .

Sighing, she turned to go in when suddenly something unexpected happened. Flying down the stairs like an arrow, Nandini came and clung to Ammaji. She managed to stop herself from falling with difficulty, otherwise they would have both been on the floor.

'What has happened?' she looked at Nandini and was shocked. Nandini was trembling and her lips quivered. She was pale with fear.

'What happened, beta? Is everything okay? Say something!' Ammaji was worried. Nandini was unable to speak. Finally Ammaji pieced together what she was trying to say: 'M . . . . M . . . Mouse!'

'*Oho*! Is there a mouse?' she asked. Nandini nodded and collapsed in a chair.

Uff. Ammaji smacked her own forehead. 'Here, drink some water. What is there to be scared of? It will go away by itself.'

'No, Ammaji! I'm very scared! Please see! Come upstairs, Please!' Nandini held on to her tightly.

Ammaji wanted to refuse. Nandini hadn't even thought about her yesterday, had she? She had never called her upstairs before, had she?

Then she looked at Nandini's terrified face and her heart melted. With great difficulty, supporting both her knees, huffing and puffing, she reached the top. And fell on to a sofa.

She isn't that bad, Nandini thought as she brought Ammaji a glass of water. She had always thought of her as Hitler. And all that stuff about having tea at five sharp, on the veranda, in that chair? Who does that? She had a child, her studies, a household to look after, Ammaji should try and understand. Now just yesterday, she had forgotten her tea. So what? She would give it today. Now because of the stupid mouse, she would have to be nice to Ammaji till Manish came back to save her.

Amidst their emotional and mental upheaval and the mouse's terror, a few days passed. Ammaji suggested many methods which Nandini tried but the mouse evaded capture. It was becoming fiercer and fiercer and Nandini more timid. Seeing Nandini's discomfort made Ammaji secretly happy but she also felt bad for her.

'Ammaji! Wait! I'll make tea, have it here, please!'

'No, beta. I will have it downstairs. With Babuji. He must be waiting for me.'

Nandini was stunned. So it wasn't some arbitrary rule made to trouble her. She began to understand some of Ammaji's deepest feelings. If she was missing Manish, how painful must Babuji's absence be for Ammaji? Ammaji must feel so alone.

Ammaji was going down the stairs, one step at a time, holding her knees, as Nandini watched her.

That night Ashu had asked his grandmother to tell him a story about herself and his grandfather. The last time she had started telling it to him Nandini had rebuked her. Now as Ammaji completed the unfinished story Nandini sat nearby, immersed in her laptop. Ashu soon fell asleep and a smiling Ammaji stopped speaking. Just then she heard a hushed voice ask, 'So, have you never had tea without Babuji?'

Ammaji was surprised. She looked towards Nandini who had turned off her laptop and had been listening to the story intently. That one moment bridged the distance between them. She shared her life's stories with Nandini, and Nandini listened.

'Thank God for that mouse! It is the reason I have got a chance to understand you,' Nandini said clasping her hand. Ammaji laughed and asked, 'I thought you were very brave. How come you're scared of a tiny mouse?'

Nandini was quiet for a few minutes.

'When I was four or five years old, my grandmother locked me in the storeroom as punishment for something I had done. When they opened the door after two hours they found me unconscious. I'm still terrified of mice.'

The fear in her tear-filled eyes shook Ammaji. What had she done? In her anger she had turned that poor child's fear into a weapon. She had let that mouse loose herself, to trouble Nandini. She was ashamed of herself when she thought of what she had done. Ammaji didn't hate Nandini, she wasn't even angry with her. She was just upset about her evening tea. If she had known that Nandini's fear of mice was real, she would never have let that mouse loose in her room. But she had been happy with the interaction between the two. What if Nandini got busy after the mouse went away? Ammaji would be left with her memories. The thought had worried her. But now it was time for her to take a decision.

She looked under the bed at the mouse, happily eating a biscuit in a mouse trap. The mouse was sort of a pet. It would come into the trap every night and she would let it out every morning. And then she would pretend to be surprised at the audacity of the mouse!

As soon as Nandini had woken up that morning, Ammaji had taken the trap to her, 'We finally caught the rascal!'

'Thank God, Ammaji!' Nandini breathed deeply.

The mouse was disposed of far away from the house. Ammaji returned downstairs and Nandini went back behind closed doors. Ammaji was restless the whole day. She wanted to chat with Nandini like she had done the previous week. She remembered how Nandini would put ointment on her knees before bedtime and how she had come to Ammaji for advice on her ethnic ware collection project, how she argued with her and how she showed her affection.

It was evening, almost five o'clock, and Nandini's door was closed. She grimaced and went and sat down on her chair in the veranda. Nandini appeared just before five, a tea tray in her hands.

'Sorry, Ammaji. Tomorrow is the last day to submit my project so I couldn't sit with you today,' she said as she put the tray down on the table. Ammaji smiled.

'Can I ask you something, Ammaji? If I were to have evening tea with you every day from now on, Babuji won't mind, will he?' Nandini asked with a cheeky smile. Ammaji felt Babuji smiling as he sat beside her on his chair. She had got her home, her position and her special evening tea back again.

AYESHA

Shabnam Gupta

It was a cold Dalhousie evening. It was only five o'clock but I could see the sun setting in the valley that lay below the cafe I was sitting in. A thin veil of mist draped over it—almost like a mother gently covers a sleeping child. I warmed my hands on my mug of coffee. The tourist season was over. All the families that had come to spend their summer holidays had returned to their homes. Only the local people remained now. They knew me well, and I knew them.

I had been coming to the Sunrise Cafe for six years now. And I always sat in this chair. If someone else was sitting on it, I would wait for them to leave. Sipping my coffee, I opened the file in front of me and looked at the first sketch.

This had been my daily routine for six years now. I sat here, drank my coffee and looked at my sketches.

My sketches of Ayesha, my daughter.

Six years ago we lived in Mumbai. I'm an artist and my wife, Madhu, a lawyer. She is very hard-working, her work never ends, so it was my responsibility to look after our daughter Ayesha. From making her tiffin and getting her ready for school, to tuition and hobby classes, I did everything. And I could make a better plait for her than Madhu. Really! When she felt extra affectionate, Ayesha would call me Dadda, and sometimes to tease me they would both call me Mom. I liked it when they did that. I liked it a lot.

Ayesha was eight when we had come up to Dalhousie for our summer vacation. We loved the mist-covered mountains and the cool breeze laden with the perfume of the deodar trees. I remember it being very crowded but we spent the whole day wandering around the town.

Madhu's work had followed her here too, but Ayesha and I enjoyed everything Dalhousie had to offer. That day she had insisted on ice cream. I had sat her down on this chair, in this Sunrise Cafe, and gone to the counter to get her ice cream. When I came back she wasn't there. I put both the ice cream cones down on the table and called out, 'Ayesha! Ayesha!' She wasn't anywhere.

No one in that crowded cafe had seen Ayesha leave from there. I looked for her, for hours, for days.

But I didn't find her.

For three months we stayed there, looking for her. Madhu had cried herself into a frenzy. She went to every temple and tied a thread at every pir's tomb. She had never believed in any of this before.

Despite the best efforts of the police we found no trace of Ayesha. The roads were deserted. The tourists had left. Madhu had finally managed to convince me to return to Mumbai.

But I couldn't breathe in Mumbai. I wanted to go back to Dalhousie. The town, this cafe and this chair owed me. And I wasn't going to let that debt go unpaid.

Deep inside I blamed myself.

I had come back to Dalhousie. It had been six years. Madhu called every day to say, 'Come back, Rakesh. I can't live without both of you.'

And I always said, 'We'll come, Madhu—Ayesha and I—we'll both come back to you.'

I made a painting of her on her birthday every year. On a large canvas I would try to imagine how she would look with each passing year. She always wore the red velvet dress she had worn that day. She would be fourteen now. Her face mustn't be as round, her hair must be longer, and the impish gleam in her eyes? Maybe? Maybe?

I would make hundreds of pamphlets with those sketches and distribute them or stick them on walls. I went to the police station every day to ask the inspector where the investigation had reached.

And then I would sit here every evening.

The owner of the cafe, Niranjan, would invariably come to talk to me, 'Is the coffee okay?'

'Hmm,' I nodded when he asked me the same question that day.

He came and sat in the chair opposite me. His eyes fell on Ayesha's sketch and he said, 'It's never happened before or after your daughter.' I didn't say anything. The sun had sunk a little lower. The mist now covered the shoulders of the sleeping child.

I looked outside over Niranjan's shoulder. A rag picker was combing through the garbage. She had a big basket on her shoulder to put her collections in, and on her chest in a sling hung a little baby. Behind her was a little five, or six-year-old girl. She said something to the little girl and picked her up.

A shock ran through my body. The coffee cup fell from my hands on the table. Niranjan looked at me amazed, 'What's happened, sir?'

But my eyes were fixed on the ragpicker's little girl. She was wearing Ayesha's dress—the red velvet dress her Nani had made for her. The dress she had been wearing that day!

'Hey! Hey! Listen!'

I ran towards the door of the cafe. Niranjan didn't know what was happening but seeing my state he ran out behind me.

The girl saw us running towards her and panicked. She must have been seventeen or eighteen at the most. She had blue eyes and a mole on her chin. She threw the stick she was holding and fled.

'Hey! Listen!' I shouted. 'Don't be afraid. I only want to ask you something.'

She ran even faster when she heard that. I ran after her and Niranjan ran behind me. She turned around as she ran and when she saw us following her she ran off the road and down a small path. She leapt like a deer down the mountain road into the valley below.

Niranjan and I chased her for quite a distance, till we couldn't see her any longer. We stopped.

It was dark, lights were twinkling in the valley that spread below us. For the first time in six years my eyes had seen a glimmer of hope.

Niranjan and I stood there for a while catching our breath. He asked me, 'Sir, this girl, is she your daughter?'

I shook my head, 'No. But her daughter is wearing the dress my daughter was wearing that day. It's torn now but I recognize it clearly.'

Niranjan looked in the direction the girl had disappeared. 'That's a gypsy settlement there, sir. We might be able to find something.'

'Let's take the inspector with us. They may not tell us but they're scared of the police. We'll go early in the morning,' he said.

I nodded again.

I couldn't sleep that night. At dawn I picked up the file with Ayesha's sketches in it and went with the inspector and Niranjan towards the gypsy settlement.

It wasn't a permanent settlement. There were fifty or sixty tents there. Torn sheets hung as curtains and some scraps of torn shamianas hung here and there. A few wood fires burned and some children roamed around. When they saw us a man came up to us. He must have been around forty and some sort of headman. Behind him came seven or eight men.

When the inspector told him about the dress, he answered angrily, 'We are gypsies, not thieves.'

The other men joined in too. The inspector banged his lathi hard on the floor and shouted at them. Out of fear they let us search their tents.

The inspector talked to the headman while Niranjan and I along with some constables began to search the tents.

We scoured each tent. I showed them all Ayesha's sketches. I told them about the dress. None of them knew anything.

I was going to give up hope when we found the girl in the last tent.

I stood outside the tent trying to gauge the girl's expressions. She was scared and tried to hide from us. Her daughter still wore Ayesha's dress.

'Look, I don't want to scare you, I just want to talk to you,' I said.

She looked at me with scared and helpless eyes, she looked like an animal caught in a trap.

'I'm not a policeman,' I said. She didn't reply. I pointed towards her daughter and asked, 'Just tell me where you got that dress from?'

She looked at me in surprise, then she looked at the dress, and then back at me. Now her face didn't have fear on it, only questions.

The people outside the tent could hear us speak.

I said again, 'My daughter was wearing that frock when she got lost. And I have been looking for her since then. When I saw that dress I thought maybe you knew something.'

I opened the file and showed her sketches of Ayesha, 'This is my daughter.'

Her eyes widened with disbelief when she saw the sketches, as if she knew Ayesha.

But then she shook her head in denial.

From behind us the headman spoke, 'Why are you frightening the girl? She's told you she doesn't know anything. Now please leave.'

The inspector indicated that it was best that we leave. I turned my back to them and whispered to the girl, 'I'm in that cafe every evening.'

We left. Niranjan told the inspector, 'The girl looks Kashmiri. Maybe they have kidnapped her too. You should check the missing persons register.'

That day I told Madhu everything that had happened. She didn't say anything but her sobs told me that she had allowed herself to hope again. I had never lost hope.

After that day I spent more and more time in the cafe. I was sure the girl would come. She was frightened to speak in front of the others, but I knew she knew something, from the way she had looked at Ayesha's sketch. I had found the first link to Ayesha.

I waited for her for several days. Niranjan came to sit with me one day. 'Sir, should we go to the settlement again?'

I didn't answer because my gaze was arrested by what I saw outside the cafe.

It was the girl. Her daughter was not with her. She came inside the cafe and up to my table. She gestured towards the file and asked, 'Sahab, are you really Asha's Dadda?'

Her words made me feel as if the universe had opened its best treasure box in front of me. I had not taken Ayesha's name in front of her. And I hadn't told her that Ayesha called me Dadda. I nodded, I couldn't speak, the words stuck in my throat.

She sat down beside me and said, 'Asha had told me about you.'

'Ayesha,' I corrected her softly. 'Ayesha, not Asha.'

She didn't hear me. She was lost in thought. Today she didn't look so scared.

I asked her name.

She said her name was Bijli and that she had been wandering from place to place with this gypsy caravan. She had come here a few months ago. These people weren't gypsies, she told us, they just joined them from time to time. When Ayesha had been kidnapped, a different set of gypsies had been here. They had kept her here in Dalhousie for some days and then sent her off with the gypsies. She had been wearing the dress then, and the two of them had been kept in the same room for some days.

My mind was in turmoil. Had the room been clean? Did they give her anything to eat? Did they mistreat her? But I didn't ask Bijli anything. I knew those questions would take me down a dark empty road from where there was no return. In the beginning I had lost my way on that dark road, and I had lost my mind. I knew that road would not lead me to Ayesha. I had started to tell myself, 'Ayesha is fine. Ayesha is absolutely fine.'

The girl told me that after that day she had met Ayesha last year. That's when she had given her the dress.

I picked up a sketch of Ayesha. 'Does she look like this?'

'A little,' she said and looked away.

I was silent.

After a while I asked, 'And you? Do you remember where you are from?'

She nodded. 'I am from a village near Udhampur. I was eight. They picked me up from the fields. This group was there then. They sent me with them. They divide up so the police don't get suspicious and they never stay in one place for long.'

'I should go now, Sahab. If anyone sees it could be the end. These people are very evil.'

Evil! My mind began to wander down that dark road again. I pulled myself back and asked Bijli, 'Don't you want to go home?'

She looked at her clothes and her rough hands, 'What home, Sahab? Who is waiting for me?'

What answer could I give her? I was her answer.

She looked at me after she asked me the question. She saw the hope shining in my eyes, she looked at Ayesha's sketch and asked softly, 'Ammi and Abba—do you think they are waiting for me still?'

Parents never stop waiting. They pray for a miracle every day. And their love doesn't diminish till they die. As she watched me I think she understood.

'I can help you,' I told her. 'The police and the women's cell will take you home. No one will even know.'

The colour of her eyes changed, first fear and then worry. She shook her head. She felt it was better to be in a known jail than believe a stranger.

I didn't want to force her. I asked her if she would come again the next day.

I went straight to the police station from there. I told the inspector everything. We checked the missing reports from the Udhampur area for the last ten or twelve years. We found a description that matched the girl, her name was Rehana.

We spoke to the relevant police station in Udhampur. We spoke to the girl's mother to get her description. She told us about the mole on her chin. There was no doubt that the girl was Rehana.

But we needed her to agree to go home. She came the next day. I addressed her as Rehana. She looked at me and wept. The old days had beckoned her. Bijli was ready to become Rehana again.

Over the next few days the police and the women's cell worked secretly to send her home.

And then the day came when with tear-filled eyes I watched Rehana sit in the police jeep, ready to be driven away.

My heart was flooded with relief; one daughter was going home today. Her parents' wait was over, their prayers had been answered.

But I wasn't without hope. There was no way that I would let the hope that I had kept alive all these years die now.

Rehana sat her two children down in her lap in the jeep. She lifted her hand to say bye to me, then beckoned me. I wiped my eyes and came up to jeep window. She handed me a piece of paper. 'Sahab, I've written the names of as many of the gypsies from the group that had Asha that I could remember. They were near a place called Manali. There is a river there and a big school. Their settlement was somewhere there. Your Asha might be there.'

I put the paper safely away. The smile on my face grew. I felt another step closer to Ayesha.

I'm coming, Ayesha, my heart said, *I'm coming*.

THE WAIT

Manjit Thakur

It was nearing the end of September but the city was in the middle of a game of hide-and-seek being played by dark rainclouds and lightening. He stepped out into the lingering hangover of freshly fallen rain.

He, Jinny, one of the most important people in one of the most famous software companies in America. Jinny, aka Girindranath.

It had been twelve years since he had left this city and Diya. Outwardly it seemed that he had come on a nostalgic visit to his home town, and maybe to fulfil his wish to see Diya once again, but deep inside somewhere all he really wanted to do was present himself to the man who had taken Diya away from him: her father, Dr Arindam Chakravarty.

Bright neon lights outside the station spelled Madhupur Junction. Madhupur had changed so much.

Girindra was reminded of his childhood when he had slept clinging to his mother, he could hear the announcements from the station. The crackling voice on the loudspeaker announcing the arrival of a train. And then the bell that rang as the train drew into the station. Three times for Up and four times for Down.

A rickshaw bell from behind him pulled him out of the ocean of his thoughts.

He had come three days ago from America. America, where he had earned money and fame. Now, his life had two ends. On one corner was Dr Chakravarty's abuse, 'You beggar, *saala bhikhari*!' and on the other, the words of the brilliant, world-famous owner of his software company, 'Guys like you can change the world!'

But during all the time that he had spent earning that money and fame, two eyes had bored holes into his back. He thought of Madhupur all the time. From where he had left, humiliated.

There was always something that pricked in his heart like a splinter. He had sworn he would only return to Madhupur when he became something, when he had enough money to buy all of Madhupur. He would become such a big man that Diya would be proud of him. Diya, whose memory had prevented him from ever getting married. Diya who was the light of Girindra's eyes. In the midst of all his success he would always think, *I wish that old man could see me now, and hear my boss's words, 'Guys like you . . .'*

Girindra wanted to show Dr Chakravarty his place. It was this Dr Chakravarty who had glared at him from behind his bifocals and ordered him out of Diya's life. Once he had left he had never found the time to return.

For some years after he left Madhupur, he had continued to write to Diya at her friend's address. But when he heard of her marriage, letters seemed useless. Now his life had two purposes. One was to ask Diya why she hadn't waited for 'Guys like you' Girindra, and the other to show that old man Chakravarty that the world had come and landed at Girindra's feet.

During his penniless days—and when he became the guy who could afford to buy a grand house on the outskirts of San Francisco—he had done some things that kept him tied to his past.

He never married. And he never thought about his family, who had thrown him out of the house at the time that he had needed them the most. But Girindra had never been able to forget Madhupur.

The Diya with whom he had sworn to live and die had faded a bit from his memory. But the glitter of Dr Chakravarty's eyes never grew dim. It always followed him. It was not for Diya but for Dr Chakravarty that he wanted to return to Madhupur. He wanted to say, 'Dr Chakravarty, the person that you had called a beggar is standing in front of you today and the cost of his suit is worth more than two months of your pension.'

He clenched his jaw. His chain of thoughts broke when the rickshaw stopped. He was standing at the main gate of his house. He took cover in the darkness. A window overlooked the road. It was open and the breeze blew the curtains. Ma had aged in these twelve years. Bhabhi was serving Bhaiya his food. Everyone was busy. The world was in place. Girindra's leaving hadn't meant anything to anybody. The neighbourhood had certainly changed. Rows of concrete houses had replaced the trees and clumps of bamboo. Halogen lights had replaced the bulbs that used to hang there. He looked despairingly at all those lights. In America he called the endless flood of lights 'light pollution'. The brain needed some darkness to rest in. But he never slept in the dark; it made Dr Chakravarty's piercing glowing eyes shine more brightly.

This was the problem from which he needed freedom. And the way was to look into Dr Chakravarty's eyes and tell him that making him worthless in Diya's eyes had been his biggest mistake.

Girindra hadn't come to this neighbourhood to go home. He only wanted to see his house. But in his heart of hearts he wanted someone to see him, and recognize him and drag him to his home. So that Bhaiya and Bhabhi, his nephew and Ma could see his wealth. He was sure his nephew must have heard about his fame. But sadly, none of the people passing him on that well-lit road recognized him. He waited—for someone, anyone. He felt as if he had everything, yet he had nothing.

Girindra had booked himself into the best hotel in town. The condition of the hotel showed him that however much Madhupur might have changed, it was all superficial. Inside, the city was the same: a ragged city that nobody came to. Why should they? He felt a strange satisfaction, a perverse pleasure. He felt good for the first time that day. Compared to that city he had indeed reached great heights.

The next morning Girindra lost his way. He found himself standing at the spot where he and Diya had met for the first time. This was the park where all the couples from the city would come just to see each other and exchange fragrance-filled handkerchiefs. And if it was possible maybe gently touch each other.

In the days when the rest of the students in Class Twelve were choosing between arts, science and commerce, Girindra and Diya had chosen each other, to be partners for the rest of their lives. When they met for the first time in this park Diya had given him a strange gift: a green bougainvillea leaf with his name scratched on it: Girin. Girindra had had nothing to give her in return except his heart. There were hardly any telephones in Madhupur at the time. Mobile phones had not made an entry in India. Sometimes Girindra would phone Diya's landline number from the STD booth.

If it stopped after three rings, Diya would know it was Girindra.

They managed to talk on the phone sometimes, but mostly it was difficult to even get to see each other. There was a sign on Dr Chakravarty's gate that read 'Beware of Dog'. Whenever Girindra had gone there it was Dr Chakravarty's piercing eyes that had filled him with dread more than the huge Dobermann.

One day it had been raining hard. Girindra was lying in his bed, struggling to compose a poem on the last page of his physics notebook.

She came home.

She, Diya Chakravarty.

He still remembered that day clearly. He had been half asleep when he felt a few drops of water on his face. He opened his eyes to find Diya Chakravarty leaning down over him, drops of rain falling on him from her wet hair. As soon as she heard he was alone at home she had come to meet him. Girindra felt the coolness of the rain and the warmth of her breath on his skin. He loved the special fragrance of her body.

He touched her face lovingly. He counted all the moles she had on her forehead, near her eyes, on her neck, her cheeks.

She had stood up suddenly and smiled at him and then she was gone. Her father would be angry if she was late. As she went she left him a letter. It was five pages long. It was Girindra's first love letter. And his last.

She asked him to get a government job that year itself. She promised to love him forever. She told him how much she loved him.

Her handwriting was beautiful. Her cursive writing in English—mashallah! Girindra had studied in a government school. She was the product of a convent school. They only taught English after the sixth standard in government schools. Girindra's English had been quite weak.

Diya's letter was filled with things of the heart, and promises to stay together. Heavy words and thoughts appeal to the head but simple things are the ones that have the gift to touch the heart. Diya's words had pierced Girindra's heart.

That letter was still safe in some file. But not all the five pages—only four. The last page, on which Diya had written that she would die if she had to live without him, the one where she had written 'only yours', that page had somehow found its way into the hands of Dr Chakravarty.

Dr Chakravarty had called him to his house the next day. He shouted at Girindra, 'Do you know that I am the biggest doctor here? In this whole town? You vagabond, saala, you beggar! You don't have enough to eat two meals a day and you will marry my daughter? Do you think my daughter will choose her own husband? And you, shameless fellow, get out from here! I will find my own son-in-law!'

Girindra's heart broke. He felt completely humiliated! But he stayed quiet for Diya's sake. Later that evening Dr Chakravarty came to his house and complained about him to his mother. 'Your son has been troubling my daughter. He is trying to influence her and if he doesn't stop what he is doing right now I will see to it that this wastrel son of yours goes to jail!'

As he left he told them that he had the police at his disposal and could get Girindra beaten up at the local police station. Girindra didn't have to go the police station but Bhaiya and his friends had beaten him up badly.

His mother had cursed him, '*Karamjala*, you have brought nothing but misfortune since you killed your father the day you were born. Now you want to destroy the rest of us!' Girindra had become unbearable for his family.

Girindra had just decided to leave the town when Diya's friend sent a message saying he was to go to her house.

Diya was there. Girindra had more pain in his heart than in all the bruises left by hockey sticks. Wounds inflicted by one's own hurt more. He felt like his family was looking for an excuse to discard him.

Diya had cooked roti and *bhindi bhajiya* for him. In a moment of love she had promised him that she would feed him bhindi. Girindra didn't like bhindi and that's why she had promised to feed it to him. He wept as he ate.

That was his last meeting with Diya. And that evening his last evening in Madhupur. He caught the night train to Delhi. He soon got a job in a software company in Gurgaon and he threw everything into it. He worked hard day and night, always thinking of new things, devising new ways. He had nothing to lose. He moved up the ladder from job to job and company to company. And finally he had ended up at his American software company where he now shone. 'Guys like you can change the world!' they had said.

Girindra returned to the present. He stood in front the imposing Chakravarty mansion. The gate was the same. 'Beware of Dog' it still said, but there were no signs of any dog. He entered the gate and a maidservant came out.

'*Ki chai?*' she asked in Bengali. What do you want?

'Dr Chakravarty?' he asked.

'*Daran*,' she said. Wait.

Five minutes passed. Girindra wondered if Dr Chakravarty would light a cigarette in the same menacing way he had all those years ago. *Will he talk about Diya? I'll offer him my packet of Havana Cigars*, he thought. *Dr Chakravarty, a gift for you*. A voice in his head shouted, *From guys like me!*

His chain of thoughts was broken when the maidservant moved aside a curtain and pushed a wheelchair into the room. He had spent twelve years of his life rehearsing the moment when he would come face to face with Diya's arrogant father. How he would show him his bank balance and photographs of his long car. The old man will probably have a heart attack when he sees my house in San Francisco he had thought.

But the twelve-year preparation came to nothing. The thought of his own greatness and the cheap pleasure he would get from fighting with Dr Chakravarty suddenly lost its appeal.

The eyes that had cost him twelve years of sleep, though still behind bifocals, had lost all their fire. They were extremely weak.

'Who is there?' Dr Chakravarty's voice quavered. The skin of his neck hung loose.

'Dr Chakravarty, it's me, Girin.'

'Who Girin?' Dr Chakravarty didn't remember him.

'That beggar. Saala bhikari.'

Dr Chakravarty was quiet. A heavy silence enveloped them. The maidservant got them some tea. Finally Dr Chakravarty told him that Diya's husband was a professor at the Jadavpur University. But despite being so close Diya never came home. She never had. It had been ten years. He had nothing left.

How pitiful Dr Chakravarty looked. And how pitiable he himself was, Girindra thought. They had both lost Diya. Dr Chakravarty survived with the help of a servant. Would that be his fate too?

Silence fell between them again. They were both deep in thought.

Suddenly Girindra broke the silence, 'Dr Chakravarty, if you don't mind, can I ask for something?'

'When I had something to give I called you a beggar. Now what do you want?' Dr Chakravarty asked with a wistful smile.

'Doctor, will you come with me to America? To my home?'

Dr Chakravarty said nothing; his eyes filled up and tears rolled down his cheeks.

THE MUFFLER

Umesh Pant

Winter had announced its arrival. As I took my warm clothes out of the cupboard, I looked among them for a muffler. It was maroon, black and white. Just looking at the muffler reminded me of the whole story. The story about how Susmit became a part of my life and who I was going to meet now.

Yes, it was winter, December in fact. Those were my wild carefree days. My mother had already declared, 'This girl has gotten out of hand now.' One day, sick of the humdrum Delhi life, I quit my job. I thought I'd spend a month travelling around and see what happened. Travelling from place to place, I found myself in Manali. I left early in the morning for Solang. When I reached the place from where the trolley took you up to Solang, a thought struck me. How about if I walked up instead? Those were the days when one did whatever one thought of.

I rejected the trolley and set off on foot. In the beginning the climb was easy enough. But as I reached higher the way became progressively more difficult. And finally, in one place the path gave way to snow.

I had been climbing over half a kilometre now and the thought of going back wasn't appealing. I broke a stick from a shrub growing on the side and began to pick my way carefully through the snow. After some fifty steps forward I froze. There was a steep, snow-covered rock in front of me. It would be impossible to climb that alone. And when I turned around I realized that going back was impossible too. My unconcern suddenly turned into fear.

What if it starts to rain? I was hanging like Trishanku on this mountain. I couldn't move forward. With every step I tried to take, I slipped, and the mud beneath the snow was giving way.

I understood that I had made a huge mistake by setting off on foot alone.

'Help! Help!' I screamed. But there was no one for miles around who could hear my plea for help. I could see the trolley high above me, ferrying travellers up and down the mountain. If one of them were to see me and realize that I was in trouble maybe I could be saved. Waving my arms over my head, I screamed 'Help! Help!' but after a while I realized it was childish. I had almost given up hope when I heard a voice calling from the valley below.

'Madam! Are you crazy?'

'Lecture me later, first help me, you idiot!' I shouted.

I looked over the ledge to see a boy. He heard this and turned to go. Oh no! He must have got offended. I felt guilty at my behaviour. Is this the way to ask for help? I had found someone to help me—and had turned him away.

'Listen! Sorry! Please help me!' the desperation in my voice increased with every word. That boy had disappeared down the mountain without saying a word. It was two in the afternoon. In a while, daylight would start to fade. Possible scenarios began to unfold in my imagination.

It would be dark soon. Slowly the cold would intensify. And taking advantage of the darkness, some wild animal would eat me. These mountains are full of leopards. And I was stuck right in the middle of a forest. No one would even find my body. This lust for adventure can have bad repercussions sometimes. Would anyone even remember me after I was dead? I think Simmi will miss me. And, yes, Ma would too. I wished I could say sorry to Papa for lying to him so that I could wander like this. I could almost see my skeleton lying among the bushes when I heard a voice from below.

'Madam?' I looked down and I suddenly came alive again. The boy had come back, this time fully prepared.

He had come armed with a rope. One end of the rope had a large hook on it. He also had a trekking stick with him. He climbed towards me carefully and soon he was quite close to where I was. He threw the rope to me. I couldn't catch it and almost slipped down the mountain in my attempt.

'Carefully, madam, don't send all my hard work sliding down the hill.'

He threw the rope towards me again and said, 'Stick the hook firmly into the ground. Come down carefully using the rope. Don't rush. There's no need to be afraid now.'

'I'm not afraid,' I lied as I moved my trembling legs towards the rope.

'Yes, I know. You must be a Lady Bond, because where do normal people like us attempt to climb steep and dangerous mountains like this without any equipment?'

He had hit home. I realized that it was better for me to keep quiet. Slowly with the help of the rope and that boy I began to descend the mountain. I was relieved. And now that the fear of death had passed I began to be aware of the cold. My teeth began to chatter. My ears and face were red from the cold.

'Here, take this muffler. Cover your ears and mouth with it.'

The boy removed the muffler from his shoulders and held it out for me. I took it gratefully and covered myself with it.

'You weren't attempting something else, were you?'

'I don't understand,' I said moving the muffler away from my lips.

'I mean suicide or something?'

He spoke without hesitation. I looked at him intently. He didn't look that annoying. I wanted to tell him to mind his own business, but that is precisely what I couldn't do. He had ruined a day of his holiday and put his life at risk for me.

'Thank you so much. If you hadn't been there today I wouldn't have been around tomorrow.'

'It doesn't matter. Thanks to you, I had a bit of an adventure myself. Otherwise I would have gone up and down in the trolley. These twists have their own charm,' he said as he exhaled and watched his breath mingle with the wind. So this was a man after my own heart after all. We would probably hit it off well, I thought happily.

He told me his name was Susmit when he left for his hotel later that evening. When I had wanted to return his muffler he said, 'Keep it as a gift from one traveller to another.'

'But you'll get cold too. And then you'll curse me every time you sneeze.'

'I don't curse. And if I remember you, well, there's nothing wrong with that.'

He looked at me for a moment as he said that. It was the first time our eyes met and I felt shy for some reason. I had to look away. The street lights in Manali bathed us both in a faint yellow glow. Maybe that's why the air suddenly became intense.

'This muffler looks good on you,' he said, and I smiled.

'Okay, then you'll have to take a return gift. I'm here for a week. Let me know if you'd like to meet up. You have saved my life after all. We should meet.'

'I have to leave early tomorrow morning for Delhi. I have an important meeting. I'll call you and we can make a new plan to meet.'

That boy was a wanderer, but not a hardened one like me. He had kind of turned down an offer from a perfectly respectable girl. We exchanged numbers and went our separate ways.

When I got back to the hotel I looked at myself in the mirror. I don't know why. The maroon, white and black muffler did look good on me. The muffler reminded me of Ma. I felt a strange excitement.

I called Ma.

'Where are you, Nimmi? You're not going to stop this madness for us, but at least let us know where you are.'

I listened to her complaints for a while and when they had been dealt with, I came to the business I had called for.

'Ma, to knit a muffler does one knit purl or knit?'

Ma was badly shocked by my question. She loved knitting and had wanted me to learn from her. She had been trying to teach me all her life. But she had always said I should learn because it's 'something all girls should know'. And I hated her reason. But today I put my hatred aside.

'You're feeling okay na, Nimmi?

'Yes, Ma, just tell me.'

It took Ma a while to return to normalcy after my question. But then she told me step by step how to make a muffler. I had decided that a muffler would be given for a muffler.

The next day I went to the bazaar where I found a nice wool shop. I bought some spools of wool and went back to my hotel. It won't take me more than two days, I thought.

'Okay, now sit cross-legged, and put the ends of the spool on each knee. And then start wrapping it from one end making a ball around your fingers.'

I remembered Ma's old knitting tutorial as I made the balls. In childhood I had barely paid attention to it but I must have learnt something.

'You know, knitting is like a relationship. Slowly, one a stitch at a time, it meshes together and grows stronger. If one stitch slips, the relationship begins to rip and all one's hard work goes to waste.' I hadn't understood what she meant then but now I wanted to understand.

'One knit, two purl.'

With Ma's words in my ears and my hands on the needles, the muffler slowly started to take shape. It was a strange madness that kept me tied to the strands of wool and the muffler that I was knitting, and a new relationship. The muffler that should have taken me two days to knit was ready by the morning. Now to see about the relationship!

Susmit had said he was leaving at eight, and it was already six-thirty. Would it be okay to go so early, just to give him the muffler? I had been awake all night; maybe I should sleep a little? Would it seem too desperate to go this early in the morning? I had doubts but was also excited about giving him the muffler. Eventually, like always, my excitement defeated my doubt.

I called Susmit's number. Once, and then again. He didn't answer. After calling four times I gave up, and just as I was putting the phone down, it rang.

It was Susmit.

'Is everything okay, Namita? You've called so early.'

'Yes, everything is fine. I've disturbed your sleep, I think.'

'No, it's good you woke me up; I would have kept sleeping otherwise.'

I was known for always having something to say. I could say anything to anybody without a moment's hesitation. But suddenly I was flustered. And a sweet hesitation had crept into me.

'A . . . Actually . . . I wanted to give you your return gift before you left.'

I said it. Susmit too seemed to be at a loss for words.

'Do you have to ask?' he replied playfully. I decided I liked his sleepy, early morning voice.

'Let's meet at seven, outside your hotel,' he said and disconnected the phone. And I slowly removed the hand that had been on my heart the whole while. This was the first time something like this had happened to me. Was this love at first sight?

Is it possible to feel so strongly for someone after such a short meeting? And this was completely opposite to how I was. I was known for not giving boys the time of day. Then what was it about this boy?

I had wasted fifteen minutes thinking and now I rushed to get ready. I even put on some make-up, which I never did. I took the perfume Simmi had given me out of my bag. 'You never know, some day the girl inside you might wake up; then you can use this!' she had said.

I wore the perfume and then Susmit's muffler. I checked myself in the mirror. I could hear Susmit's words in my ear, 'This muffler looks good on you.'

I thought he would like the muffler I had made for him. I had stayed up the whole night for something after a long time. He had not bothered about his life for me, so what was losing a little sleep? I stepped out of the hotel.

I waited for a while. It was cold. Susmit's muffler and thoughts of him kept me warm.

Just then a car came towards me and drew to a stop. Susmit sat in the driver's seat. Next to him sat a little girl. My mind went into a tumult on seeing the girl. And then I looked at the back seat where a definitely married girl, around our age, sat.

The car stopped and three people got out. Susmit smiled and introduced us.

'This is the girl I told you about.'

I stood in silence. I didn't know what to say. Then Susmit pointed to her and said to me, 'She chose the muffler you're wearing now.'

I pasted a false smile on my face to hide my feelings. Had I fallen in love at first sight with a married man?

'Oh! Your wife has really good taste. You're a lucky man.'

They heard me and burst into laughter.

'I'm not that lucky. The lucky man who is my brother is over there at the ATM.'

I was at a loss for words again. But I liked this twist in the story.

After talking for a little while I gave him the muffler I had made for him and came back to my hotel.

Even before I reached the hotel there was a message, 'Thanks for the muffler.'

'Same to you!' I wrote back.

And leaving future possibilities for the future for now, I lay down in my room. I had a whole day to catch up on my sleep and a whole lifetime to fulfil my wishes.

ACROSS THE SEVEN SEAS

Ankita Chauhan

There was a nip in the air. From under a blanket of clouds the sleepy, pale morning peeked in from the window. My half-open eyes were full of dreams. Dreams that Vinay had shown me that evening.

'Start packing, my Elizabeth, we are going to Canada sooooooooon!' All those o's expressing his happiness. I was happy. Life had been kind to me these last eight months.

After twenty-two years of travelling between Rajasthan and Noida, I, Reva, was going abroad for the first time. Life was going to step out of the realm of the usual and dance to a new music.

During this time Vinay had changed everything: from the sandals I wore to the ringtone on my phone, Enrique's 'Let Me Be Your Hero'. There were lots of parties. While he was basking in the congratulations of his friends for his two-and-a-half-year project in Canada, I was looking for a few moments of peace, rather, some courage.

Over and over again, my fingers would go to the contact list on my phone and stop. I wanted to talk to Ma. I wanted her to know how happy her daughter was. I was proud of my decision to marry Vinay—a decision I had taken against society's dictates, a decision that Ma had not agreed to despite thousands of pleas. The mantle of society's meaningless rules that shrouded her mind was the source of my uncertainty.

The crux of that confusion stuck in my throat and I told Vinay about it later that night—about the fear that was growing in my heart. When I told him about going home, he had closed his laptop and said, 'Do whatever you feel is right,' and turned off the night lamp.

Suddenly it felt as if all my relationships were drifting apart. His turning his face away and his monosyllabic answers with his back turned told the story of his relationship with my mother. But the burning silence of the night had filled me with courage. I had decided that I would meet my mother once before I left the country.

The next morning the unshed tears in my eyes must have melted something in Vinay. Breaking a mouthful from the parathas on his plate he said, 'I didn't say no, yaar. Go. If you want, I'll take you. If Ma doesn't let me in I'll pitch a tent in the garden.'

He laughed and ate my burnt parathas as if they were the best jalebis in the world. I could only look at him with a teary smile. He had never let the acid of Ma's words tarnish our relationship.

My mind slipped back to the day I had first taken Vinay home to meet Ma. After sitting with him for a little while she had taken me by the hand and pulled me into the kitchen.

'He has been raised by some NGO, his education paid for by charity. He has no home, no people—'

'It wasn't charity, Ma, he won a scholarship. It isn't easy to get them.' I cut her off mid-sentence. She stared at me for a while and then in an angry gesture she turned off the gas. The tea that had been on the stove for him hadn't even had time to come to the boil. Like his relationship with Ma.

'Your father isn't here any more, so you can do what you want,' she said and stormed out of the kitchen. It felt as if someone had closed a tight fist around my heart. I think Vinay had heard the bitterness of her words. He left the house without saying anything.

I had never dreamt that life would lead me to this sort of crossroads. I couldn't get Vinay's face, stripped of its smile, out of my mind. I couldn't stop him even though I had wanted to. Something was stuck in my throat.

For the next few days I struggled to breathe, and I chose the person who would walk beside me, not direct me. I proposed to Vinay. We moved to Delhi after getting married. Despite everything, a day had not gone by when I hadn't thought of Ma. The conversation with Vinay that morning gave me strength, and finally I dialled the number on my phone with trembling fingers.

'Hello,' I heard Ma's voice.

'I want to meet you, I'm leaving the country next month.' The words stuck, my throat was dry, I felt like crying, but I didn't. I listened to the silence on the other end of the phone for a long time.

I had tried many times to talk to her over the last few months. I had tried to explain, but the silence that had crept into our hearts scraped and echoed. When the bonds that run in our blood become estranged, emptiness fills our chests. I didn't want to leave the country with that emptiness, and that's why I had reached out to Ma for the last time.

The next morning we were at the Nizamuddin Railway Station. Vinay had managed to get two tickets on the Jan Shatabdi. It hadn't been easy to get them at such short notice but he had managed somehow to get me a seat. By one-thirty that afternoon the train was speeding along. He stood near me. I clutched his hand.

'Water?' he asked. I shook the water bottle next to me. I looked at him for a while. 'Why can't this train be going to a place where everything is as we want it to be?'

'Crazy girl,' he said and caressed my hair.

'When I was small na, with Papa . . .' I stopped: there wasn't really anything to tell him that I hadn't told him before—over and over again. Things like how I often travelled with Ma and Papa by train. Ma would make alu-poori specially, on his request. Sometimes she would sing for him. She would pull his hand towards her and pretending it was a mic she would sing, *'Ab toh hai tumse, har khushi meri.'* I would always get emotional at that song.

'Do you want to eat bread pakoras?' his voice broke my reverie. He had noticed the sadness on my face.

'Ma was never like this when I was younger. Really! Everything changed after Papa passed away. She stopped laughing. It was as if she had locked herself up somewhere and forgotten,' I spoke haltingly. For the rest of the journey, Vinay stood with my hand held tightly between his.

A little while later, we were both in my town, in the courtyard of my house. I looked at the house carefully. Then I saw Ma standing in the doorway, behind the curtain that fluttered in the breeze. My heart grew heavy.

Memories were strewn around that courtyard: the small hand pump in the corner and the broken pots in which flowers grew. Everything was the same. Nothing had changed, except the tulsi plant that had wilted, like Ma's face.

I stood like a stranger at the entrance of my house. I was waiting for Ma to come to me and, like the old times, shout at me. And then, like the old times, hold me tight to her heart. But Ma didn't come. Ma who once had counted the seconds for me to come back from college, who didn't sleep a wink when I was sick, today sat far away, locked in a room. As he filled water in the bottle from the hand pump, Vinay asked me softly, 'What should we do?'

By then I had stepped into the room that was filled with Ma's silence. The memories held me, but Ma didn't move. She was sitting on the same stool near the window. She hadn't looked at me then, and she didn't now.

Vinay had sat down on a chair in the room. I didn't say anything to Ma and went straight into the kitchen. Once again I put some tea on the stove for Vinay. Once again my heart thudded with fear, wondering if Ma would accept him or not. I was putting cardamom in the tea when I heard the sound of footsteps.

I turned around to see Ma leaving the room and walking towards the stairs. For a while I stood with three cups of tea. Then, disconsolately handing Vinay a cup, I followed Ma.

She was sitting on a mat on the roof. In a corner stood a cupboard that held an entire childhood: a broken bat, the invention that I had started to make with papa with parts from a video game . . . Memories came alive.

I saw a sigri in the corner. I pushed it towards her and said pleadingly, 'Ma, you know I never get to eat bajre ki khichri in the city.'

'Don't trouble me, just go,' Ma said.

'Don't do this, Ma,' I said moving closer to her. Our shadows met but the relationship stayed aloof behind locked doors.

'You children can do what you like, isn't it? You did what you thought was right. The matter is closed.' Ma got up and went downstairs. I sat there for a while under the stars, collecting bits of scattered memories.

The night deepened. Ma had left me surrounded by questions when she had left. For the first time in eight months I felt as if I had done something wrong.

I don't know what I had thought when I came here. *If my being here is causing Ma pain, I'll leave. Maybe my absence will give her some peace*, I thought as I went downstairs. Every step seemed to be taking me away from myself. My legs were trembling.

I saw that it was eight-thirty. The train for Delhi left at eleven. My mind was heavy. Ma sat on the string cot out in the courtyard. Memories do fade with age but Ma had deliberately swept away all memories of me.

I picked up a few things and, without looking at Vinay, said, 'Come! Let's go. We'll wait at the station.'

'What do you think I am? Come here, go there?' I stopped, startled. I looked at him and went into the kitchen. This was the first time Vinay had spoken to me like that. It was my fault. I should never have brought him here.

A tear rolled down my face. I remembered that Vinay hadn't eaten anything all day. I kneaded some flour and while I made the rotis, memories of Ma flooded my mind again. My mind fought with my heart. I made two birds out of the flour and put them on the *tava*. Ma used to make them to placate me whenever I got angry with her.

A sob rose in my heart. I quickly put my childhood on a plate and took it to Ma. I put that plate down in front of her with so much hope. She looked at the plate and then at me. She said nothing but her eyes filled with tears. Not wanting to cause her more pain I went back inside. I wanted to fill myself with Ma's fragrance before I left. Just then I heard Vinay's voice.

'It's amazing, I'm the one who is hungry and your daughter gives you the plate! No matter how hard a man tries, a girl's first love is always her mother.' Ma turned away at his words.

This last effort had failed to melt Ma's stubborn heart. I wanted to grab Vinay and go far away. I was moving close to him when he stopped me with a gesture and looking straight at Ma he said, 'This stubbornness of yours has made my life hell. I can't fight with her, I can't say anything to her because she doesn't have the option of running away to her mother's house. And I feel you sulk on her behalf too, because she seems to have forgotten how to sulk. I had fallen in love with a life-filled girl; today she is just a lifeless puppet.'

I was shocked. What was he saying? Was he angry with me too? I was embarrassed. Ma's worried eyes looked for me. I stood, scared, hiding behind the curtain.

Vinay, now sitting on the cot near Ma, said, 'Now you tell me, Mummy, I don't know what you have taught Reva. But apart from noodles she doesn't cook anything. How can I eat noodles every day?'

Oblivious of her anger Vinay looked Ma in the eye and spoke to her like an older man. I had told him once that no matter how angry she was with me she could never tolerate anyone else saying anything bad about me. I now understood what his game was. My eyes filled with tears but I was smiling. He carried on.

'We are going abroad for three years now. She weeps the whole day, where will Ma stay? How will she stay? I said let's take Ma with us so she said Ma has refused.'

'Refused? I can refuse only if she asks me!' Ma finally broke her silence and glanced at Vinay. I looked bewildered from one to the other.

'She's going away for three years. If she had been a son, wouldn't she have at least asked me to go with her?' Ma said.

'Look at that, she didn't even ask you and just made it up because she was scared to ask you.'

'This girl, she used to trouble me like that too,' Ma complained.

'Do something, Mummy. Please come with us. She'll starve me to death in Canada.' Vinay said. While all this was happening Ma had gone into the kitchen and put her pot of choice on the stove—the *kadhai*. Within seconds the smell of roasting semolina filled the house. Ma's heart was like a piece of ice which Vinay had melted with the warmth of his affection.

We were leaving on a new journey the next month. Flying high amongst the clouds, Ma was telling Vinay about how crazy I was in my childhood. I was smiling. My country was getting left behind. I felt a stab of pain at the thought. But I was happy. I was taking my home with me.

A BIRD IN FLIGHT

Snehvir Gosain

The highway was more or less empty. The white car speeding along it was approaching Alipur. The passenger, Shivshankar Sahay, seemed to be ill at ease. As the car raced towards the town, so did his heartbeat. Suddenly the car moved onto a dirt track. He placed his hand on the driver's shoulder. 'Ram Dayal, please stop the car.'

Shivshankar stepped out and stared at the track for a long time. His son, Akhilesh, got out too. 'What are you looking at, Papa? Hurry up.' As soon as Akhilesh reached him Shivshankar said, 'Akhilesh, do you see that dirt track? It goes to Aldausi. We used this track to go to school.' Annoyed, Akhilesh replied, 'Arre, Papa! You got down just for this? Come quickly now. I don't want to stay for more than one day. If we get late, we won't reach before nightfall.'

Shivshankar felt heavy-hearted as he climbed back into the car. He stared at the track until it disappeared from view. A few unfinished pages of his past were scattered

201

there. He was surprised that Akhilesh couldn't see anything there. Children who grow up in the noise of the city don't know how to read the silence of villages and towns. He used to come to Alipur every year, but this time everything was reminding him of something.

He remembered when Amma had come to the city for the first time. As soon as she put her first step in the one-bedroom flat she had said, 'You left that huge house for this hovel?' How could he have explained to her that it wasn't the house that he had left but the environment that had stifled him from his childhood till his youth? As he grew older it had all started feeling like undeclared fetters to him. After finishing college in Delhi, he had never considered returning to Alipur to settle there. Amma had felt really bad that her son had preferred to spend his life alone in the city instead of with his bustling family at home. Now when his own son didn't want to visit Alipur, he understood his mother's pain.

The sky now wore a mantle of vermilion. The sun was hiding in a mango orchard towards the west. Those mango orchards held some years of his; he wanted to investigate those too before he left. Throwing up mud along the narrow lanes of the town, the long car finally stopped outside Sahay Villa. Getting out of the car Akhilesh said, 'Ram Dayal, please take the car to the hotel. Papa, come, I've given the keys to the guard. He'll get it cleaned up in the morning.' As Shivshankar looked at his house with brimming eyes, a few memories slipped from them and rolled down his cheek. He steeled himself and bid his house goodbye. Tomorrow his house would become someone else's forever.

Shivshankar's ancestral home was to be sold on the eighth of August. It needed to be sold because there was no one left to look after it. He had been putting it off for some years now. He came every year, got it cleaned up, plucked guavas, which were now a challenge for his teeth, from the tree in the courtyard. While his mother had been alive she had come to see them in the city. As she sat there cutting guavas she would say, 'Your children will never understand the taste of guavas grown in your own courtyard. They never get holidays in the guava season.'

Shivshankar always felt that his mother was very unhappy with his having moved to the city which she expressed through metaphors of guavas and mangoes. Shivshankar's children had never understood the taste of rice grown in their own fields, or how to make a slingshot to break raw mangoes from the trees, or how to catch the fish that came into the fields with the monsoon.

There was a well near his home in the village. His grandmother would build a wood fire near it. Even after all these years he could savour the taste of the *litti-chokha* in his mouth. When he had left his house his father had said, 'Son, remember that to fly high in the sky you have to uproot yourself.' He felt that his father had foreseen this day all those years ago. On the eighth of August the uprooting of Shivshankar would be complete. The only person who felt pain because of that was Shivshankar.

Akhilesh's voice pulled him back into the present. 'Papa, get up. We have to deal with the stuff inside the house.' The new owner wanted the house empty. In fact, he didn't want the house at all. He planned to tear it down and build a new one. They had organized a sale to get rid of the old shisham furniture. Shivshankar couldn't sleep. He hated staying in a hotel in his own Alipur. The soft mattress poked. Shivshankar's pain reached his voice; pleadingly he asked, 'Son, won't you think about it just once more?'

Akhilesh's heart melted when he saw the tears in his father's eyes. He explained gently, 'Papa, we have been putting it off for so many years because of you. Now we are spending more in the house's upkeep than its worth. It's for the best that we sell it.' He was explaining things to Shivshankar the same way that Shivshankar had explained why he couldn't have an ice cream when Akhilesh had been small. Akhilesh's childhood had been left behind, and Shivshankar's was returning.

They left in a while and soon, after a short drive down bumpy village roads, the car drew up near Sahay Villa. All the furniture had been placed outside. The old shisham dining table was there and on it served for Shivshankar was his whole life. This was where he had eaten his first morsel of food. This was where his mother would coax him to eat his food. It was at this table that he had announced his decision to move to the city and where he had fought with his father. He put on his glasses to read the price put for it: fifteen thousand rupees. Shivshankar thought the price was low for a lifetime of memories. He moved ahead sadly.

Just inside the doorway was large hall. At the far end of it, his father's portrait still hung on the wall. His father looked angry, as if he were saying, 'See, Shivshankar, I told you, didn't I, that if you run from your home, you'll never belong anywhere?' He heard a voice calling from the kitchen, 'Leave him alone now, let him go. He has his own dreams too. Even if he stays his heart won't be here.' It was as if his memories were coming alive and he could watch them like a play. Akhilesh called from outside, 'Papa, come out, there is a lot of dust there. You'll fall sick.' Shivshankar called out hurriedly, 'I'm coming, just give me a little time.' He was wondering if the house would remember him once it was sold to someone else. Would all traces of his life be forgotten? He picked up a small book stand from the pile of furniture. His father used it to read the *Ramcharitmanas*.

Suddenly the room echoed with his father's voice: Everything must end and dissolve into the five elements. He tried to convince himself, but his heart wouldn't listen. He held the book stand to his heart.

Carrying the book stand, Shivshankar went outside again. He was reciting verses from the *Ramcharitmanas* and the *Gita* softly. The furniture was all being bought. He went up to Akhilesh and said, 'Do you know? Your Dadaji used to read the *Ramcharitmanas* and the *Gita* from this book stand.' Akhilesh had his mind on other things. Distractedly he said, 'That's all okay, Papa, but now the wood is all rotting. What will you do with it? Leave it there, please.' Shivshankar held it even closer to his chest like a stubborn child in the shops insisting on an expensive toy.

As he stepped out, four men went into the hall and, using a step ladder, started taking down the large chandelier. Shivshankar smiled as he watched them take it down.

That chandelier was just ten years younger than him. It had come all the way from Hyderabad just to light up the occasion of his tenth birthday. Now after years of service it was being retired. In a sense it was just some wood and iron that was being sold but that wood and iron were witnesses to Shivshankar's whole life. Amma and Pitaji's hands had often touched those things. Their touch was still present in these objects. It's only the body that grows old, not feelings. Shivshankar felt as if the light of Amma's love and the glow of his father's face still shone in those things. His eyes were filled with memories of days past and tears of pain. He couldn't stop the tears. He wept and smiled; sun and rain played together on his face.

Just then he heard loud voices from behind him. A handkerchief covering his face, Akhilesh was on the phone, 'I said give the phone to Kapoor Sahab. Hello! Yes, Kapoor Sahab. How are you feeling now? The thing is we have done all the paperwork here. I wanted to get it registered today itself. I've fixed everything in the tehsil office as well. Now I'm going to have to wait till tomorrow. If you weren't able to come you could have at least informed me.' Shivshankar understood that the buyer, some Avinash Kapoor, was unable to come that day. He was immediately refreshed by a feeling of contentment. He had just received an extra day to gather his memories.

Akhilesh had returned to the hotel. Shivshankar had insisted on staying behind and now he stood gazing out at the temple near the fields with a feeling of emptiness. Surdas' verses were being played on the loudspeaker.

The sound of a car stopping broke his reverie. Ram Dayal had returned after dropping Akhilesh. He came and stood next to Shivshankar. Shivshankar gestured towards a tree at the back of the house. 'Do you see that tree, Ram Dayal? It's a Mirzapuri guava. My Dada Sahab had planted it and guess who he gave the watering duty to? Me! And when I refused you know what he said?' Ram Dayal watched an emotional old man get even more emotional. Shivshankar looked at him and said, 'He said, if you water it yourself the fruit will be sweeter. It was not something I understood in my childhood. I raised that tree like a child. Now you tell me, won't I love it? How I can leave it forever?'

Ram Dayal had no answers for the old man. Instead of comforting him he asked him a question, 'Sahab, I am a poor man. I went to the city to earn money. But why did you leave?' Shivshankar smiled, 'In youth a man runs, Ram Dayal, and in his old age he returns.' Ram Dayal didn't understand. He was in his running days. Home . . . The place the word conjures up is the place you will always call home, the place where you left behind some important part of yourself. The rest are all stops and resting places. Shivshankar's self was in this old house in Alipur, where his childhood swung from an old guava tree.

As they watched, the mango orchard swallowed up the sun again. As the night deepened so did his bleakness. Some stuff still lay about the hall. Before he could go into his room to inspect his youth, his phone rang. It was Akhilesh. 'Papa, it's late. You haven't left yet?'

The thought of leaving his house sent a shiver of pain through Shivshankar's body. Appealingly he said, 'It's the last night, son, let me stay at here, at home, tonight.'

A lot had changed in Alipur, but the nights were still as dark as they had been all those years ago. Shivshankar was asleep in his room that adjoined the living room of Sahay Villa. He was awake. He had come every year but had never slept in his own room. There were twelve hours left for the house to go so he had asked for his bed to be made in his own room. He didn't want to sleep. He wanted to live the twenty years he had spent in this house again in those twelve hours.

His tired body fought his tired mind for a long time, but in the end the tired body won and he fell asleep. In his dream he saw his father, and that lake in which once he had almost drowned as he played. He saw his father watching him from the other end of the lake. His mother was working but never took her eyes off him. As he swam he reached the middle of the lake. Suddenly he began to drown. His father watched him but didn't come to save him. He was alone. His eyes jerked open. But his body lay asleep.

He saw his whole life around him. He saw himself fall off his bicycle while learning how to ride and the whole family administering to the tiny scratch. He saw the preparations for a party when he came first in the ninth grade. He saw his father angry and himself with a suitcase in hand leaving for the city. His mother was trying to blink away her tears. The last thing he saw was the slight smile that lit his father's face when Akhilesh was born. He had spent his whole life desperate for that smile. Shivshankar felt his hold on time loosening. He didn't feel the loneliness any more that he felt sitting by the window in his apartment.

Everyone stood on the other edge of the lake: his father, his mother, his wife. They were calling him to them. He only had to cross that lake. But he wasn't able to swim. He was drowning. There were a few hours left till daybreak. Shivshankar was exhausted. Slowly he sank below the surface. He felt himself close to his parents. His breath slowed.

It is dawn. Shivshankar is in a deep sleep. The temple bells are ringing and, over the loudspeaker, Surdas' verse can be heard.

My mind, limitless, knows no joy
A bird in flight, it returns
To the mother ship, ahoy!

A NOTE ON THE CONTRIBUTORS

Ankita Chauhan is from Sawai Madhopur in Rajasthan. She has written over twenty stories for radio. She blogs about books at soundingwords.blogspot.in and tweets @_ankitachauhan.

Shabnam Gupta went on to do an MBA after graduating from Sophia College, Ajmer, with a BA in English. But she continued to write poems and stories in Hindi and published them on her blog. In 2014 she joined Neelesh Misra's Mandali. Her stories have appeared on Big FM's *Yaadon ka Idiot Box*, Red FM's *The Neelesh Misra Show* and Saavan's *Kisson ka Kona* and *Time Machine*. She is a senior writer with Content Project Private Limited and blogs at sophiashab.blogspot.in.

Snehvir Gusain is a teacher who enjoys writing stories. His characters are a means to understand himself. After studying mass communication he took to writing to express his creative impulse. He has written over sixty stories for

211

Neelesh Misra. 'Jahaaz ka Panchi' is one of his best-loved stories.

Anulata Raj Nair has an MSc in chemistry. She lives in Bhopal and is an active blogger. In 2014 she joined Neelesh Misra's Mandali and has written over 150 stories for various shows including *Yaadon ka Idiot Box*, *The Neelesh Misra Show*, *Kahani Express* and *Time Machine*. Her poetry appears in the acclaimed collection *Ishq Tumhein Ho Jaega*. Her stories, cover stories and nazm are carried regularly by various publications. She is the associate creative head at Content Project Private Limited and blogs at allexpression.blogspot.com.

Chhavi Nigam has a PhD in political science. She teaches at a university in Lucknow. Her stories, poems and other writings are featured regularly in various newspapers, magazines, websites and blogs. She has published two collections of stories and received the Pride of Women award for literature. She has written sixty-five stories for *Kisson ka Kona*, *The Neelsesh Misra Show*, *UP ki Kahaniyan* and *Time Machine*. She is a senior writer with Content Project Private Limited. She has also worked as a translator for the Lucknow-based rural newspaper *Gaon Connection*.

Kanchan Pant is a writer and journalist. After seven years as a TV journalist she began to write stories for radio. She has written over 200 stories for *The Neelesh Misra Show*, *Yaadon ka Idiot Box*, *Kisson ka Kona*, *Kahani Express* and other shows. In 2014 she published the story 'Bus Itni Si Thi Ye

Kahani', authored her first book of short stories, *Bebak*. She has been awarded the Hindi Yuva Pratibha Sammaan, and the Golden Paper Award by the Indian Literary Society, Singapore. In 2016 she was named one of the fifty leading writers of Uttarakhand. She is the creative head at Content Project Private Limited.

Umesh Pant is from Gangolihaat in Uttarakhand. He has a Master's degree in mass communication from Jamia Millia Islamia. He is the author of the popular travelogue *Innerline Pass*. He began his career as an associate writer with Balaji Telefilms, Mumbai. Soon after, he started writing stories with Neelesh Misra. He is a roving writer with *Gaon Connection* and writes for several Hindi newspapers. He also works as an onsite Hindi linguist with Google for Magnon eg+. He has written several films and songs for radio. He has two websites, www.umeshpant.com and www.yatrakaar.com, and tweets @umeshpanthy.

Jamshed Qamar Siddiqui is a writer and journalist. After many years as a TV journalist he began to write stories for radio. His romantic and humorous stories for *The Neelesh Misra Show* have won great appreciation. Jamshed has also written scripts and dialogues for TV serials. He writes for *Gaon Connection* and is associate creative head with Content Project Private Limited. He tweets @jamshedhumd.

Manjit Thakur is a journalist. After receiving a diploma in journalism from the Indian Institute of Mass Communication, he studied at the Film and Television Institute of India. He has worked with *Navbharat Times* and DD News. He is the author of *Panch Vanchit Ilakon ki Reportage* and *Ye Jo Desh Hai Mera*. He has also translated books by V.S. Naipaul and A.P.J. Abdul Kalam into Hindi. He has written thirty-five stories for *The Neelesh Misra Show*. He works with *India Today*.